Cha Cha's Rainbow End

"There are sore spots which never cease to be sensitive; wounds of the spirit which never heal."

—Edgar A. Guest

Cha Cha's Rainbow End

Jerry Brown Schwartz

Published by Deeds Publishing in Athens, GA
www.deedspublishing.com

Printed in The United States of America

Cover design and text layout by Mark Babcock

Artwork by Bill Garrett
All other artwork (pp. 48, 61, 76, 129, 167) by Michael van Tonder

This is a work of fiction. Names, characters, businesses, places, events, locales, and incidents are either the products of the author's imagination or used in a fictitious manner. Any resemblance to actual persons, living or dead, or actual events is purely coincidental.

ISBN 978-1-947309-35-7

Books are available in quantity for promotional or premium use. For information, email info@deedspublishing.com.

First Edition, 2018

10 9 8 7 6 5 4 3 2 1

"Some people are masters of the put down, delivered in a way that can seem incidental, harmless, but with results that can linger on for a lifetime."

—Roger Housden

Contents

Acknowledgments

I am grateful to Danielle McKlveen for the many hours of typing and making sense of my late-night longhand writes, and rewrites.

And Lois Wisen for her great edit that really brought Cha Cha forward, and made her shine.

Once more to Harry for being my sounding board, and his insight.

To Bob and Mark Babcock and the people at Deeds Publishing for bringing my book together, and making me proud.

Dedication

I would like to dedicate this book to some extraordinary women who helped shape me into the person I am today.

My maverick Grandmother, Monty; my Charleston dancing, harmonica playing, forthright mother, Dorothy; my kind hearted, fun loving sister, Polly; and my card playing, laughing, good time great aunts, Azzie and Dessie. All the above are looking down from heaven.

To my always fashionable 100-year-old Aunt Beautiful Aunt Bea and my world traveling gorgeous cousin Gloria.

To my book loving sister, Colleen, who I may call in the middle of the night to ask, "Would I place a comma here?" and my 99-year-old joyous, always of good spirit Aunt Willie.

And, as always, to my husband, Harry, who encourages me to reach all my goals, and reminds me, "it's 2:00 am in the morning," when I am still writing into the wee hours.

You are all my treasures.

CHAPTER ONE

It's My Turn

Cha Cha braked her peach-colored woody station wagon to a stop. She grabbed the hammer lying next to her on the car seat and got out. The tool felt natural in her grip. She smiled and let her mind wander to her father, and spoke as if he stood next to her. "So often I stood, awestruck, watching you skillfully wield this hammer." Running her fingers over the handle, she admired its patina, worn and shiny from years of her father's sweat. She approached the mailbox with its rainbow paint faded from years of weathering, and went to work.

She tapped at the rusted hardware holding it in place. Staccato metallic strikes broke the quiet of the early morning. Stubbornly, the old mailbox held on; it did not want to surrender its perch. With

each swing of increasing force from her hammer, the earth seemed to vibrate. The set-upon mailbox finally trembled, then let go. Cha Cha watched the old mailbox fall to the ground. She paused, put both hands on her chest, took several deep breaths, and closed her eyes. Suddenly, she was five years old again.

"Cha Cha," she heard him say in his soft, controlled voice, "let's make sure we get all the colors of the rainbow." She remembered how he moved his stepstool so she could reach the box. Putting his hand over hers, he guided her brushstrokes, leaving vivid arcs of red, orange, yellow, green, blue, indigo, and violet. Cha Cha shivered with delight as each stroke of color made the rainbow come to life. Father was precise. "We must not miss a color," he said.

She mused a bit longer. His voice sounded kind, his words full of love as he spoke her name. She did not recall his voice ever being raised to her, but in the night she often overheard the quarreling voices of her parents. She could only guess why her father didn't stand up for her against her mother's harshness. *Stop it,* she chided herself. *You are in transition, and it feels splendid. Enjoy this moment and all the ones you will create in your new life.*

Opening her eyes, Cha Cha shivered and brought herself back to the present. She picked up the mailbox and thought, *I can search for happiness. I know my future will not be like my past. My new life will be happy, full of love and full of life. I will say, "You there! I am Cha Cha, and you are…?"* Cha Cha looked at her unadorned left hand and wondered if any man would want to put a ring on her sizeable finger.

CHAPTER TWO

Mother's Story

Cha Cha's mother and father married late in life. Already in her forties, Cha Cha's mother, Jolean, was a tall woman with straight posture. She wore dark clothes that concealed her large bosom, that is, except on Sundays when Jolean was a sight to behold. She dressed from hat to toe in complementary petunia colors, from white to purples. On those days, wearing a fitted suit with a peplum that emphasized her small waist, pencil skirt that showed slim legs, white gloves, and shoes that matched her suit color, Jolean was a striking woman. Others described her as mighty handsome. And, indeed, she was.

Jolean dismissed the attentions of many, but her father believed his daughter needed a provider for her golden years and decided she should be wed. Then, he and his wife would be free to pursue their own dream of moving to a western state.

Jolean wanted nothing more than to remain with her elderly parents, but this was not to be. When the word got out, new suitors serious about marriage came knocking at her parents' door to invite the fine-looking Jolean to dinner. Her parents vetoed each one until a friend arranged for Jolean to meet the well-to-do bachelor, Mr. Vickery.

An only child, Mr. Vickery inherited a home and a large parcel of land after his parents were killed in a car accident. A hard worker and a perfectionist, he turned the land into a lucrative herb and Christmas tree farm. He was handsome and tall with fine features that suited his slim build. He was overly neat with impeccable "Yes, ma'am" manners and a sterling reputation, though his shyness kept him single long past his desire to be married.

Mr. Vickery tipped his hat when he passed Jolean on the road as she walked to church every Sunday morning, a habit she would continue throughout her life until she became bedridden. He asked a neighbor about the prettily dressed woman. He was too shy to mention her physical beauty, never mind approach her. When a suitable occasion arose to meet Jolean, he accepted a dinner invitation at her parents' home.

Mr. Vickery believed it would be nice to come home after a hard day in the field to a beautiful wife, a spotless house, and dinner on the table. After calling on Jolean several times, it was decided the two should wed. Even though she had recently turned forty, her parents still ran her life and the arrangements with Mr. Vickery were made. Her father turned a deaf ear to Jolean's desire to remain a spinster and to accompany her parents when they moved. The mature bride to-be wept as she left the only home she had ever known.

A few months after the joyless wedding, having submitted to the dutiful responsibilities of a wife, Jolean was horrified to learn she was pregnant. Her husband, whom she regarded as an unwelcome stranger, took delight in the upcoming birth. He tried to pamper his reticent wife, although she wanted no part of his attentions. Jolean withdrew, becoming numb to her surroundings. After the birth of their daughter, Jolean wanted little to do with the child or her husband. Out of necessity and his natural kindness, Mr. Vickery stepped in to "mother" the baby girl.

"How lovely," Jolean's mother said to her husband at the christening.

"I told you so," he replied. "Our daughter is now a proper married woman. Thank goodness she now has a decent, responsible husband, a healthy child, and a home. She will be fine."

"I don't know...did you see her eyes? I have never seen more ill-fated eyes."

The reluctant new mother named her child Charlise Charmaine after her father's mother. The delighted new father, cooing at the happy little red-haired baby, shortened the name to Cha Cha. Offended, Jolean objected in a huff, "How could you? That's a name for a tart! I will not allow my daughter to carry such a name!"

Mr. Vickery quietly asserted himself without confronting his wife's protests. Eventually, she conceded with ill grace and called her daughter by her full name only when scolding her. Motherhood did not come easily and her pretty mouth settled into a permanent straight line.

One late afternoon, Mr. Vickery came in from the garden to find his wife kneeling on the floor, scrubbing with feverish determination as the neglected, red-faced infant screamed in her crib. Frightened, he crooned to his child as he bathed and fed her. The baby fell asleep on his chest as he rocked her, keeping her steady with his hand on her tiny back. He rocked well into the night, deep in thought out of concern for his child's welfare.

The next day, after spending hours at his workbench, he fashioned a comfortable, workable sling for the baby to ride in while he worked around the farm. Thereafter, Cha Cha joined her father as he did the unending tasks required at the herb and tree farm. She happily gurgled at the smell of freshly turned earth. He talked to her throughout the day, explaining all that he did and why. She seemed to enjoy his chatter, even when he recited the Latin names for all the herbs, and he reveled in finally having a nonjudgmental listener.

Cha Cha grew into a beautiful toddler with captivating dimples and auburn curls that shone bright red in the sunlight. Her huge brown eyes took in everything. Her father fashioned larger carrier slings as his child grew. He made a piggyback-style harness from a discarded backpack. The two were literally inseparable.

Each night after feeding, bathing, and putting his little girl to bed, he took his own bath. At this time, Jolean would go into her daughter's room and gaze at the beautiful little being she had borne.

How curious, Jolean thought, that she felt so little for her own child. At arm's length, she admired the long lashes that swept down toward her baby's cheeks, the creamy shine of her skin, and astonishing curls. Where had that color come from? No one in her family had hair that color. Disturbed by the stirring of a nameless emotion deep within her, she eased out of the room before her husband completed his bath. Fascinated by her unanticipated feeling, Jolean went in when she could do so unobserved. Only she knew the content of her private words to her child. No one heard the questions she asked herself, or the words she spoke to her baby while observing her, but no outward loving bond showed from her actions toward her child.

Other than her interest in antiques, Jolean kept to herself except for Sundays at the Baptist church. Even then, she never developed any close friendships with the congregation's women, and despite regular attendance, the church's teachings provided her no solace.

As Cha Cha grew and began to observe the world around her, she started to ask her father questions. "Why don't we go to church with Mother?"

"Your mother prefers to go alone." Seeing his daughter's questioning look, he added, "Don't worry, Cha Cha, we have the largest church of all—nature. We can pray anywhere, under a large oak or seated in the middle of Christmas trees with a blue sky overhead. The animals are right with us."

At home, Cha Cha listened in to pleasant conversations between her parents. Though they never touched, there were moments of peace that reflected their inherited gentility. When she could, Cha Cha included herself in these talks; it was one of the few enjoyable times the family shared. She was allowed to ask questions and cleverly kept the talks going for hours.

To fill the hours in her day, Jolean cleaned and never grumbled about the many household duties that needed her attention. The furniture stood polished and free of dust. She pressed and laid out her husband's clothes. Meals were on time; however, the food she prepared had little spice because smells from most anything irritated her. When she did rest, she read the Bible for pleasure and did not share her knowledge or thoughts.

In the orderly household, all things had a proper place. Jolean had decorated with elaborately detailed furniture that belonged to the distant past. Cha Cha would run her hands along the shiny smooth polished wood and wonder why her mother put so much attention into the house, and so little attention on her. There was no artwork to speak of and few pictures on the walls. One year, Cha Cha made a frame at school, sized to fit a picture of her father. He placed it on his dresser and she liked to believe he treasured it. When not working, her father studied herbs, made healing salves, and grew the best looking Christmas trees in Georgia. If either of her parents had dreams of a different life, they were silent on the subject.

CHAPTER THREE

Growing Up

The years passed and while the bond between father and daughter strengthened, the tenuous relationship between husband and wife grew ever more brittle. When he dared to suggest that his wife use the herbs he so painstakingly cultivated to improve their meals, she took offense. "I will not have those odd, aromatic, weedy herbs in this house." Her face would get red and her voice would get higher in pitch. "It's bad enough," she would say, "that I consent to cook those collard greens whose odor makes the entire house smell." Thereafter, the food continued to be savorless, eaten by three people in silence at precisely the same time each day.

Throughout Cha Cha's childhood, the family's daily routine stayed much the same. Their breakfast started with lifeless, perfunctory greetings. Cha Cha waited for her mother to sit first. Her father took his place at the head of the table. Breakfast rarely varied. Their morning meal consisted of one fried egg, a slice of toast, a bowl of plain oatmeal with a tiny bit of cream, and two cups of coffee for the adults, one with hot milk, the other black. Cha Cha was served a glass of milk.

Cha Cha would often look up from her bowl of oatmeal thinking, *I wonder if my parents ever show affection toward each other. I've observed other couples smiling at each other when they come to our farm to buy things from us. They hold hands and pick up their children with love and laughter. Why are my parents different?* This question plagued her at other quiet times. Why didn't her parents get along?

Jolean saw the bond Cha Cha had with her father and feared the two would form an alliance against her. Still, he was respectful of his wife when Cha Cha asked, "Why doesn't my mother love me? She is never happy with me. Please, Father, what do I do wrong?"

Even though Cha Cha's father could see she was hurting, he replied, "Cha Cha, you must never speak ill of your mother. Now run along and do your studies."

As time passed, the atmosphere in the house tightened with tension. The strain was evident, especially when both parents were in the same room. Their forced politeness locked them into solitude. Cha Cha longed to get around it, but didn't know how.

Lately, though, she'd started to overhear muffled sounds of mutual scornfulness coming from behind their closed bedroom door at night. Afterward, she would hear the bedroom door open and close, then the heavy tread of her father's footsteps in the hall.

Her father had set up a bed in the dayroom, which had been created when he'd glassed-in the side porch. He slept there most nights. The low light of his lantern cast a glow that crept under Cha Cha's bedroom door. She pretended not to notice that anything was wrong.

When Cha Cha arose for school, the dayroom was neatly put back together. Her father would sit in grim silence having coffee alone at the table. One morning, Cha Cha ran to her father, threw her arms around him and declared, "I love you bigger than the sun!"

Her father gently pulled her arms away and said, "Thank you for that. Now ready yourself for school." Cha Cha looked up into her father's face. She saw a single tear run down his cheek and worried she made her father unhappier than before. As she dressed for school, she thought of a pitiful starving dog they had once seen on the road. She begged her father to stop, but he kept going. At this moment, she felt like that poor old dog—empty and alone, with no one to intervene and say, "Don't worry child. I love you. Everything will be all right." She tried to put the thought out of her mind by finding gratitude in her full tummy and warm school clothes.

Cha Cha's nightly prayers were long, pleading to God for her parents to find happiness. She prayed that her mother would not be so disinterested in her, and would find peace in the Bible, and her father, in his gardens. It didn't occur to Cha Cha to pray for some happiness for herself.

One morning, after hearing her parents argue into the night, she watched from the front window and saw her mother walking toward the Greyhound bus stop. She was gone for hours. That afternoon, a delivery van from a local antique shop pulled up in front of the house. Cha Cha gasped in astonishment. Her mother, who rarely left the house, had gone into town and purchased a bed, a dresser, and a rocking chair. Uniformed deliverymen moved the parlor furniture to the attic and put the furniture her mother had purchased into the old parlor, apparently now her mother's bedroom. Cha Cha watched as the room took shape. However, with the stormy look on her mother's face, she dared not ask questions. Her father came in from the gardens. He sized up the situation and his face tightened.

"So be it," he said. He turned and walked away without another word.

The chill that permeated their home turned into the silence of a deep freeze. Pushed farther from her mother's coldness, Cha Cha gravitated toward her father.

Cha Cha immersed herself in schoolwork. She was diligent in her studies, and shone academically in school. Though the other students respected her mind, they never picked her to be on their ball teams or gave her more than a casual nod in the halls. Cha Cha was tall, and that made her feel awkward, as if she didn't fit in, but she glowed inside when someone asked her to explain something they didn't understand.

During a team competition in history class, she correctly answered each question directed to her side of the room. The reward was no homework for a week. Her team burst into cheers when she scored the winning points. Afterward, Cha Cha thought her classmates would come to her in friendship. Her acclaim was short-lived. No one seemed to recall beyond the day when her correct answers gave them the prize. Her classmates didn't invite her to join in their fun.

Her father, sensing Cha Cha's unhappiness, decided he would take her to see a movie once in a while to cheer her up. Her mother disapproved, denouncing the sin exposed in the movies. He took her anyway, and on one special Saturday a miracle occurred. Her father took her to see *Gone with the Wind*. It was as if heaven and earth had moved on her behalf. Cha Cha watched transfixed. Her senses were overwhelmed with the scope of color, human drama, and passions played out on the huge screen. Her father, anticipating that Cha Cha would pepper him with questions about the Civil War, had studied up and prepared to answer her queries. To his surprise, she said nothing. She was quiet all the way home as her mind spun with a flood of long suppressed emotions.

The next morning at breakfast, Cha Cha asked

her questions. "Mother, did Father ever kiss you like Rhett Butler kissed Scarlett?"

Her mother's dropped fork splattered egg yolk when it hit her plate. Color burned on her cheeks and her eyes narrowed. Cha Cha's father was speechless. The two parents looked from Cha Cha to each other. Her mother recovered and turned to Cha Cha. "No more movies for you!" she exclaimed. "Now you see why I don't approve. You clearly can't see the difference between make-believe and real life. Hurry now. Your father can't wait forever to drive you to school. Besides, you should be walking for exercise."

Cha Cha's mother abruptly stood and cleared her half-eaten meal with a sharp clatter of dishes. She whirled around and shook her finger at her daughter. "Shame on you! Your father has serious work to do."

Hurt by her mother's response, Cha Cha turned to her father for support. "Finish your breakfast, Cha Cha," he said. "There's time." Cha Cha could have sworn she saw her father suppress a grin as he raised his coffee cup and winked at her. "I liked the movie, too," he whispered.

Shortly after, Cha Cha sat in the station wagon, waiting for her father to take her to school. Staring out the windshield, she indulged in a daydream where her mother followed her father out onto the porch and kissed him goodbye, then added loving, caring words like, "Have a good day. See you for supper, darling. I'm cooking your favorite tonight." At this, her father grabbed her mother for another kiss before jogging down the steps, his handsome face aglow. Her mother stood on the porch and waved as they drove away, a loving look upon her face.

The heavy station wagon door clunked shut and interrupted her fanciful daydream as her father settled into the driver's seat. Cha Cha's words tumbled out in a rush. "Father, we will go to the movies again, won't we? And I love it when you take me to school. It shows all my classmates how much you love me, to take time out of your busy day for me." She prattled on. "Isn't it a magnificent morning? Will we be trimming the herbs today? They smell so good after washing them and laying them out. Tomorrow, the herbs will be ready to bind and hang up to dry. They'll be ready for your next batch of salve."

Her father sat quietly until she wound down. Then he said gently, "Cha Cha, remember, showing off changes the experience for you. I love you, and that's what's important. Yes, we will go see another movie. Now, be diligent in your studies today. Ask lots of questions."

Cha Cha wondered, *why doesn't Father give me a big hug? Tell me my life will be okay? Why?* Instead, she replied, "The teacher often praises me. Anyway, it doesn't matter what those silly girls and boys say, or if they don't like me." Cha Cha stopped talking and withdrew into herself as her father started the car. Still, she felt pleased to sit next to him.

When he braked to a stop in front of the school, Cha Cha was reluctant to leave. She asked, "Father, may I walk home today? The bus is so noisy."

"Okay," he answered. "But don't tarry at the creek. Your mother will worry."

"Mother worries about me?"

"Yes, Cha Cha. Everyone shows love differently. No one ever really knows what's in a person's mind or heart. Now, run along and make me proud."

These words came from her father so she willed herself to believe them. "Thank you for the ride."

As the station wagon pulled away, she felt alone and, for a moment, panic made her heart race. Taking some deep breaths, she watched the car until it was out of sight. Then she squared her shoulders and walked toward the jumble of students milling around in front of the school waiting for the bell.

At every opportunity, Cha Cha stopped at the creek, no matter the weather. Often she would take her shoes off, stick her feet in the rippling water, and daydream about a loving mother, father, sister, and an annoying little brother, camping trips as a family, and a shiny, bright red bike. *Sorry, Father, I will stop at the creek. I have to. There is something important here for me.* Cha Cha's anxiety spiked as it always did whenever she perceived her aloneness, and the creek cooled not only her toes, but her burning thoughts of what a family could be. She felt oneness with the birds that flew overhead, and the animals that scampered in and among the brush, including the creepy crawlies that wandered onto her sleeves. She vowed to one day surround herself with people and pets that would thrive with her loving care.

Covertly, Cha Cha observed her classmates. She didn't fit in, and other than towering over her classmates, she wasn't sure why that was the case. She consoled herself, casting off her doubts of being accepted by her peers, and instead sought the approval of her teachers. She worked hard to make a special place for herself through scholastic excellence and her teachers expected no less.

Even with her focus on learning, her mind wandered in class. Something stimulating would often grab her attention. Today was such a day. Vaguely, she heard her science teacher call her name.

"Charlise. Charlise?"

The teacher's voice seemed to come from far away. Cha Cha came to with a jolt as she felt the teacher's hand on her shoulder. Looking around, she realized every eye in the classroom was on her. Cha Cha's face turned red and blotchy, and she squirmed in her seat.

"Charlise, are you back with us?"

"Yes, ma'am."

Sensing Cha Cha's discomfort, the teacher asked, "What's caught your attention? Maybe you could share it with the rest of the class."

Cha Cha's desk was beside the window. She eyed a large praying mantis as it sat motionless on the other side of the windowpane. "Well, ma'am, it's that." Cha Cha pointed to the extraordinary insect.

The teacher addressed the class. "Everyone gather around. Charlise is going to tell us all about this fascinating insect."

The teacher meant to make an example of Charlise's daydreaming, favorite pupil or not. Chairs scraped back and the students, delighted with the interruption of a boring class lecture, crowded around Cha Cha's desk. Exclamations grew loud in the small classroom. The teacher shushed her students, then said, "We are listening, Charlise."

> *"The good stars met in your horoscope and*
> *made you of Spirit and Fire and Dew."*

— Robert Browning

Cha Cha's face, now animated, became beautiful. Her creamy complexion returned.

From that moment, the teacher's prepared lesson was forgotten. Cha Cha knew all about the praying mantis. She pointed out its grasping, spiny forelegs that were held together as if in silent meditation. "But the mantis is a fierce hunter biding his time while he appears frozen in prayer. He is ready to reach out in a flash to catch his prey. Why, I even read once that a mantis killed a hummingbird!"

The students gasped and stepped back from the window. Cha Cha smiled at their squeamish reaction to her nature lesson. The students became absorbed in their impromptu subject and asked question after question, which Cha Cha answered. Even the teacher was impressed with Cha Cha's ready knowledge. Taking advantage of the momentum from her fired-up students, the teacher told them to write a theme on the insect they found most interesting.

As a result of what proved to be a profitable learning experience, the teacher set aside classroom time for Cha Cha's Corner. Once a week, Cha Cha introduced a new insect. The class came to enjoy the fascinating creatures, and their roles in gardens and the environment. Entomology opened up new worlds as knowledge displaced fear.

Cha Cha's finest hour came when her teacher made arrangements for a class field trip to her father's Christmas tree farm. Cha Cha stayed up most of the night before the event making muffins for the entire class.

"Charlise," her mother said, "leave my kitchen spotless and clear out that smell."

Her mother's extreme state of nervousness could not dampen her spirits. Cha Cha lined up baskets of perfect, tempting muffins on the sideboard and the kitchen shone before she went to bed. When she awoke, to her surprise she found the muffins had been placed on her mother's beautiful silver trays, and pitchers of raspberry Kool-Aid were set out on the porch table. Knowing her mother's peculiarities, Cha Cha decided to accept the kindness and say nothing.

The field trip was a miraculous day. She was proud of her handsome father and his knowledge of farming. The students gained a heightened respect for their quiet classmate. For a day, the hole of loneliness in her chest felt healed. Cha Cha would later recall the day's events, including her beautiful mother's gesture, as one of her favorite memories.

This event inspired Cha Cha to begin journaling about her daily accomplishments. She would tiptoe into her mother's empty room and leave her folded, detailed notes on the pillow. The air in her room held a light sweetness, like lavender, which Cha Cha found odd since her mother loudly proclaimed her dislike of herb smells.

CHAPTER FOUR

Dreams of the Future

The exception to the family's schedule took place on Sundays when her mother would dress in one of her pastel suits that reminded Cha Cha of water color paints. There were pinks, yellows, blues, and violets, with gloves, shoes, and pillbox hats to match. Cha Cha couldn't figure out exactly when her mother purchased these lovely suits. Otherwise her clothes were a field of monotonous grays or black, the same drab colors she picked for Cha Cha to wear. Her mother walked to the local Baptist church. Cha Cha never inquired as to why her mother never took her along, or why her father didn't drive her mother to church. Instead, she was profoundly grateful for the time, a few precious hours she could spend with her father.

Leaving the house behind, they would head for the inviting lure of the gardens. During this special time father and daughter shared, he would acknowledge the love he held for her in his own comforting way.

Cha Cha realized the garden presented an escape for her father as well as herself. During their breaks from the gardening, the two would sit on straight-backed chairs in front of the garden house. It was pleasant to be in his company, even in silence. She felt happy when they would share a talk.

He let Cha Cha paint the plain chairs a bright yellow. To her delight, he then painted ants, ladybugs, and sweat bees up the legs and across the lattice backs. A dragonfly perched at the top, while a tomato hornworm curled around the bottom of one leg.

"I like being tall like you, Father," Cha Cha said. "People say I favor you, except of course for my hair. I like that I resemble you."

He looked over at her and smiled. "Your auburn hair is pretty. My mother's hair was the same color. My father and mother died in an accident just before your mother and I were married."

"Father, do I look like your mother, besides my hair?" Cha Cha was intrigued. She had never seen any pictures of her grandparents. Her father never spoke of them and she wondered what his childhood had been like.

"Well, she was smart, kind, and pretty, just like you. Let's go back to the garden now. Lots of work to do today."

Cha Cha reveled in each of these conversations. Sunday mornings felt different somehow—relaxed, brighter, free. As she gathered her tools, Cha Cha said, "Father, our time together is my greatest treasure. I will hold it in my heart forever."

It wasn't usual for Cha Cha's father to dig deeper for her feelings, but he noticed her face had turned from happy to downcast. "Why do you look so troubled?" he asked.

Cha Cha wiped away tears with her sleeve. "I feel sad that I can't make Mother happy. I dream of the three of us, laughing, hugging, and taking long picnics by the creek."

"I understand."

The two set about their chores, flowing in the well-practiced harmony of having worked together for years. Her father patiently taught her his extensive knowledge of the herbal healing properties. He would focus on one herb every Sunday morning, from cultivating to applications of healing, cooking, and storing. Cha Cha learned how to make his healing unguents, salves, and tinctures.

"Father, do you remember how you helped Mr. Dempsey's boy? You stopped his bad cough with your special herb tea. Everyone was so worried, and now he plays outdoors. I saw him riding his horse. Do you believe I will be able to help people heal someday?"

"Yes," he said, "I believe you will. You have a talent others don't have and I'm sure you will use it for good."

Together, under his instruction, they smelled and tasted the herb in its dried and fresh forms. He had her describe the herb in all its aspects, mentioning how he favored a child's view. His prompting made her feel important and she shared her opinions with him. She reflected on the contrast between her mother's domain with its mercilessly scrubbed house full of antiques, and her father's bountiful gardens full of life, wonderful, diverse smells, flavors, fragrant dirt, singing birds, and interesting insects that buzzed around, one minute here, the next gone.

After one teaching session, her father leaned forward, resting his elbows on his knees, and looked at her. "Cha Cha," he said, "you will one day wander on a journey of love, laughter, and fulfilled dreams. Everything you long for is out there waiting for you. I know this with all my heart." He paused to look skyward. "There will be a rainbow's end for you. You are of a different nature than most. You see the world beyond the obvious. Others miss that. You are blessed."

As her father stood to resume the care of his gardens, he gave her a rare show of affection and kissed her on the top of her head. She absorbed her father's vision, a future filled with love and fulfillment.

Looking ahead in time to the day she might find a special someone else who understood her different nature, Cha Cha visualized Scarlett in Rhett Butler's arms. At eleven years old, romance seemed a long way off. Distracted, she picked up her basket of garden tools.

Mr. Levy, their neighbor and part-time employee on her father's tree farm, interrupted her reverie.

Cha Cha greeted him, "Mr. Levy, it's wonderful to see you. How is your family?"

Mr. Levy never ignored her, unlike some grownups who discounted children. His kind, soft eyes and gentle manner made her feel good.

"Thank you for asking, Cha Cha. The family enjoyed those muffins you left on our porch Sunday. They are so good! Nobody else thinks up your unusual combinations of ingredients. We'll taste test your new recipes anytime. Happy to do it."

Cha Cha's cheeks dimpled as she smiled.

"Thanks! See you, Mr. Levy."

She picked up her basket of tools and headed toward the greenhouse with a light heart. Mr. Levy found her father, and the two men left to prune the Christmas trees into a perfect shape that would bring holiday cheer for the customers and cash to run the farm for another year.

Cha Cha particularly loved working with the evergreen seedlings in the greenhouses, which needed attention year-round. Her father supported the family selling herbs and vegetables, healing concoctions, and after Thanksgiving, Christmas trees. The bounty of their gardens not only provided sustenance for their family, they benefitted many others. People swore by her father's healing salves. His reputation was known far and wide. When added up, the family lived well on the income generated by her father's efforts.

Cha Cha was fascinated by the holidays when carloads of laughing families came to find their perfect Christmas tree. Her attention constantly leapt from her chores to the families bustling around the tree lot. She watched as excited children shouted to their parents. "This one! This one!" Mothers shepherded their unruly children through the forest of trees while fathers picked up their laughing, squealing little ones and swung them high into the air, their faces shining with love. The intoxicating smell of freshly cut evergreens seemed to make everyone giddy with holiday cheer.

It wasn't unusual to hear high-spirited children burst into song with "O Christmas Tree." Others would join in the merriment and she heard them talk about how they would decorate. Cha Cha was mystified. *How odd it is*, she thought, *we sell all these Christmas trees and even ship them out to strangers halfway across the country, yet we don't put up a tree in our own home. Mother probably doesn't like the smell.*

Her mind continued on its path of thought. *Mother believes in Jesus' birth, so shouldn't we celebrate Christmas, too?* Then Cha Cha remembered overhearing her mother say, "All this fuss with presents, trees, and such, has nothing to do with the birth of Jesus. Nothing."

The scene on the tree lot made Cha Cha both happy and sad. *This is how it should be*, she thought as she watched a trio of cheering children jump up and down as their parents purchased their trees from Mr. Levy and her father. *There should be joy, especially now. Where is ours?*

She knew that something was terribly wrong in her home. Silent questions flooded her mind. *Why don't my parents hug or kiss me? Aren't children supposed to know how to love?*

Cha Cha found no answers. Having turned to mockery, the happy bedlam before her made her stomach ache and her chest tighten. She turned away from the scene and headed deep inside the greenhouse, away from the windows overlooking the tree lot. She wanted to hide from her troubled spirit. It appeared other children didn't have her concerns, which made her feel singled out as if she had done something wrong. Searching her mind, she recalled her father's prophecy and believed that somewhere, someday, she would find her rainbow's end. She didn't wish for a pot of gold. She did wish that next season, when she woke up each morning and saw her face in the little mirror over the bathroom sink, there would be a smiling, happy person looking back at her.

When no one could hear, she talked to her precious baby seedlings. "Where will I find my rainbow's end?" She watered the cedar seedlings and touched each one to feel their delicate new life. Cha Cha loved the responsibility of nurturing these rooted babies. She looked forward to the day when the seedlings were big enough to be set free. Still, she felt for them, relating to the awesome plight of going out into the world, knowing the tiny plants would face the power of the earth: rain, lightning, storms, maybe even volcanic ash. Most would survive to become a perfect tree, but what of her release into the world when she grew up? How would she weather her search for a happier life? The seedlings would stay where they were planted and not have the choices she would have to make.

Her father broke her deep thoughts as he opened the greenhouse door.

"Hi, Cha Cha, I overheard some talk in here. Are those seedlings good listeners?"

She smiled. "Yes. They sure have grown these past weeks."

"What do you say about sitting and sharing a muffin before we head to the house?"

"Oh, Father, that would be nice."

CHAPTER FIVE

Something's Cooking

C ha Cha's father loved muffins. To please him, Cha Cha perfected a muffin recipe using cookbooks checked out from the library. She experimented with ingredients on her own until she was satisfied with the result—truly fine, melt-in-your-mouth muffins.

She augmented her recipes with the herbs grown at the farm. Combining her father's superior knowledge of healing herbs with her culinary skill made for a muffin that not only tasted good, but was better for health than an ordinary muffin. Her father could identify the herbs used in the batter from the delectable aromas wafting off the muffins as they cooled on the sideboard.

Her mother was vocal about those same aromas. "I clean the house all day long to get rid of cooking odors, and then Charlise bakes and makes the house smelly again."

Cha Cha did her best to avoid her mother's comments by making sure the floors and counters were spotless after a baking adventure lest she be banished from the kitchen, as her mother often threatened to do. Cha Cha regretfully set up a fan in the window to pull the mouth-watering scent of baking muffins out of the room. *I wonder if there's something wrong with Mother's nose.* The impudent thought made Cha Cha giggle, even as she diligently labored to remove all trace of her baking.

She continued to absorb her father's knowledge of herbs and

applied it to creating muffins with specific ingredients, in particular, adding certain ones for elevating moods. She experimented in finding the right mix to help her father find happiness, and when she didn't see the positive results she hoped for, she asked him, "Will I ever know enough to heal people's sad and ill spirits?"

Her father considered the question. "Cha Cha, a person must want to be healed first. If they choose to be sad and ill, no magic potion or medication on the planet will make them otherwise." He walked away, giving her neither the answer she wanted, nor the praise she craved.

The next morning over coffee, her father sensed Cha Cha's gloom. He said, "Cha Cha, since your classmates and the neighbors like your muffins, how would you like to set up a table next to my garden shed and start selling muffins tomorrow to our Saturday customers?"

Cha Cha was thunderstruck. "Oh, yes, Father!" Her mind kicked into gear. "The muffins will look more tempting with cellophane wrapped around them, and I'll tie each one with a pretty ribbon. Father, can you take me to the market? I'll need some things, and I'll need to take some money out of my bank account. And I'll need cellophane, a few baskets, some labels, pens, poster board to make a sign and…"

"And an accounting book to track every penny of income and outgo," said her father.

Her mother listened in and said, "It would be a waste to start such a venture. And I'll not have my cupboard raided. Every ingredient will have to be purchased by your profits."

Pressing her hands together as if in prayer, Cha Cha pleaded her case. "You have my promise, Mother. The kitchen will be left clean, and I'll pay for all the ingredients I use. Please?"

Her mother raised a finger, but before she could protest further, her father banged his fist on the kitchen table.

"Seriously, Jolean, what would it hurt?"

He returned his wife's glare with a stare of his own that Cha

Cha had never seen. Cha Cha's astonishment at her father's support turned to wonderment for another reason. It was rare for him to speak her mother's name. Her mother inhaled sharply, turned on her heel, and left the room.

Compassion welled up in Cha Cha's throat for her embittered mother. *Maybe, just maybe, some of the healing essence from the herbs will find a way to Mother's heart and she will smile. Father allows for things to unfold. Please God, let this be!*

Cha Cha went right to work and baked muffins well into the night.

Bright and early the next morning, Cha Cha was startled to find a new roll of cellophane, a basket of satin ribbons cut to the right length, labels, and an accounting pad placed next to her breakfast plate. She didn't inquire how they arrived or who brought them. A wave of emotion flowed through her. When it subsided, she wrote the herbal ingredients, the date, and "Cha Cha's Muffins" on each label. She liked the look and feel of the colorful ribbons as she tied them in bows atop the wrapped goodies. She smiled with pure joy, admiring each muffin as she completed her task.

Her father painted a table with leftover sunshine-yellow paint. He placed the table beside the garden house so all the herb and tree customers would have to walk past her "muffin shop." Cha Cha was thrilled.

"Well, this is your first day as an entrepreneur," her father said as he helped set up the muffin stand. "I suggest you offer samples of each kind. Once they taste the muffins, I bet you'll sell out. They'll come back next week to buy more." Her father looked at her with confidence, and his kindness spilled over her.

Cha Cha burst with joy. And as it turned out, her father was right about the samples. She sold out of muffins before lunch, and even took a few orders.

When her table was clear of inventory, Cha Cha ran to tell her father, who was busy with customers in the herb garden. As usual, he counseled his customers on the proper use of the herbs according to the desired result. She waited until he was finished before she rushed up to him. "Father, oh, Father! This is the most wonderful day of my whole life! Please, Father, may I sell my muffins every Saturday? I sold everything, and they want more, and I have customers, and we all had so much fun!"

Her father smiled and nodded his assent. "I'm so proud of you! Your mother thought this was a frivolous endeavor, but how can she argue with your success? Be sure to leave your mother a thank-you note for the ribbon and such. And yes, you may sell your muffins on Saturdays. I'll help you set up your accounting sheet. After all, now you're in business."

"I promise, Father, I will write a nice note for mother."

Cha Cha went to her room and wrote a heartfelt note to her mother. She tucked it beneath her mother's pillow with a corner out where it would be seen. From that day forward, her mother shared her kitchen and Cha Cha made good on her promises.

Cha Cha's happiness about her brilliant success in the muffin business was tempered by the sadness on her father's face. She noticed lately how her father, who had always been orderly and precise, failed to clean his garden tools or put them away. Once, he left his planting record book in the cornfield. The more evidence she saw, the more she felt panicked. Not knowing where to turn, Cha Cha thought to consult with Mr. Levy. Perhaps he had also noticed something wrong. First, she decided to bake a batch of double dark-chocolate muffins. When she presented one to her father, he raised his eye-

brow, as it was he who had taught her that dark chocolate raises the spirits. He accepted the muffin and went about his day.

Cha Cha doubted the muffin would work its cheerful magic on him as he seemed so sad. He had cared for her all these years and taught her knowledge of gardening and being responsible. Now she felt helpless to give him the care he needed. Nor was she aware of any recipe that could improve her parents' joy for one another.

Her troubled mind roamed as she continued with her chores, trimming rosemary. In a thoughtless moment, she rubbed her eyes, spreading the strong essence. It irritated her senses and made her eyes water. Sad tears didn't feel any better and they hurt your heart.

She heard the approaching roar of Mr. Levy on his small mo-

torbike. Mr. Levy was such a dear neighbor, a man with the kindest eyes in the whole world. He was not only a part-time employee and her father's good friend, but someone she felt she could trust.

"Hey there, Cha Cha," he said as he pulled up near her and got off his bike. "How are you?"

Cha Cha knew when Mr. Levy asked, "How are you?" he wanted to know. She stood up from her trimming and didn't hesitate. "I'm concerned for my father. Have you noticed he stands for a long time staring at the heavens? When I ask him what he's looking at he gets angry and tells me to go back to my chores. Please, Mr. Levy, what can I do to help him?"

Cha Cha knew Mr. Levy wouldn't ordinarily comment on another family's business. As he gazed into Cha Cha's troubled eyes, he stroked his chin and replied, "Dear girl, we can get confused about the world we live in and how we feel about life. You have to understand that in matters of the spirit, even adults can't always help one another. It's not your role to help your father or mother. They are your protectors."

"That can't be, Mr. Levy. We're here to help one another—all of us!" Her grief rose to the surface and this time, real tears spilled. "Nothing in this mean world makes sense."

Mr. Levy laid his hand on her shoulder. "I'll try to talk with your father, maybe even suggest he make an appointment with my doctor. It's up to him. Your father is a very private person."

"I thank you from the bottom of my heart. You are my only friend."

They both looked across the field at the sound of her father's tractor. Mr. Levy said, "A young girl should not be concerned with these heavy thoughts. Get some play in." He mounted his bike and turned toward her. "Cha Cha, suppose I ask your parents if I can give you a puppy. Our Daisy recently gave birth, and we have four perfect little ones in need of homes. Are you ready to care for a pet?"

Cha Cha's face lit up and then, as quickly, her gloom returned. "Some things I do know, and no matter how cute the puppies are, I know there would be no room. A dog would jump on furniture, run through the house, play under the dinner table. It would be an intrusion and would upset my parents. So thank you, but no. I would love it, but I know my parents would never consider it."

"Maybe the situation will work itself out. Sorry I mentioned it."

Mr. Levy handed Cha Cha a clean handkerchief he retrieved from a pocket in his overalls. He got on his motor bike and left, sending a cloud of newly plowed earth into the air behind him.

"Thanks anyway, Mr. Levy." Cha Cha called out, but he had disappeared from view.

She gathered her clippers and basket, and upon reaching the garden house put her tools away. As she sat in her yellow chair, she heard the hum of her father's tractor headed up to the barn. Despite

Mr. Levy's advice and good intentions, her young heart felt heavy. She closed her eyes and tried to think good thoughts.

Eventually, her father walked up and said, "Nice of you to wait for me. Why do you look so sad? Did you finish trimming the rosemary?"

"No, Father, I put away my tools. I couldn't focus my attention today, but I'm okay now that you are here."

He furrowed his brow and strolled into the garden house where Cha Cha was sure he had hidden a bottle and would drink. When he rejoined her, he said, "We should hurry. Your mother will be waiting on us for dinner."

At the table, Cha Cha asked questions to break the uncomfortable silence.

"Charlise, can't you see your father does not wish to talk. Now finish your meal—no need to help with the dishes tonight."

"I don't have much of an appetite anyway. Mother, may I be excused? Goodnight, Mother, goodnight, Father. Sorry I didn't finish trimming the rosemary. I will get to it tomorrow."

CHAPTER SIX

A New Reality

Cha Cha awakened early on Sunday. This special day always meant together time with her father when he would share his knowledge during their chores. She held fast to every minute. She had no reason to believe this glorious Sunday morning would be any different, especially with the sun's brilliant rays casting warmth on all of earth's living creatures.

Cha Cha sat alone at the huge oak table waiting for her father. As usual, her mother had eaten early and gone to church. Cha Cha pouted. It seemed they wouldn't have breakfast together as they always did. She enjoyed their lively chatter. His coffee cup was unused. Believing he was tending to an early chore, she finished her toast, oatmeal, and milk, but before she could search for him, she heard his shuffling feet as he entered the room.

"Father, why didn't you have breakfast? Would you like me to pour your coffee?" He did not reply. Something in his demeanor made Cha Cha feel shaky.

He said, "Sit for a moment." He took her hands in his. "I am glad you are my daughter," he said. That was it. Cha Cha yearned for more words of value. "Now go, the rosemary must be trimmed."

Her hands trembled, and she had a sudden urge to hug her father. His shoulders seemed thinner than she remembered as she pinned his arms to his side. She took in the scent of his skin, a mixture of trees, herbs, and soap, which remained in her memory long after he walked away. She followed him outside.

"Start your work," he said as he walked toward the barn.

Cha Cha stood transfixed. The sun's rays brightened the greenery on the perfectly laid out herb beds with not a weed in sight. She stood motionless; her view of acres of evergreens stretched out as far as she could see. To her right, there were several fields of tall corn-rows with stalks like fringed Palomino horsetails moving with the breeze. Cha Cha soaked in the sun's warmth as if it was fuel for her soul. She started clipping the rosemary.

Cha Cha didn't know why, but today her heart was racing. *I can hardly breathe. What's wrong with me?* She felt frightened, more afraid than she had ever been in her short life. To calm herself down, she took special care to trim the rosemary as perfectly as her father would had he been the one doing the chore. She tried to focus on her work, but for an unknown reason, the usual pleasure of her chore escaped her.

She waited, assuming her father was still in the back field. She had seen Mr. Levy walking through the rows of Christmas trees. *He will meet up with Father. The two always stop and chat,* she thought. She lay on the soft dirt and put her rolled-up sweater beneath her head, feeling the sun's warmth on her face. "This feeling of doom is silly. Father is fine," she said to herself.

In the distance, she overheard Mr. Levy whistling as he worked his way through the rows of Christmas trees where he checked each one for imperfections. All sides, up and down each branch he worked, trimming away dead areas and shaping them for the future. He also maintained her father's high standards. She watched him. Each time Mr. Levy paused, his whistling stopped. He turned his head this way and that, and cupped his ear to hear something Cha Cha could not make out.

Mr. Levy put down his tools and walked away. Cha Cha followed out of sight. She heard the low rumble of her father's tractor and when Mr. Levy increased his pace, she saw the tractor was smack up against a tree. A limb lay across the tractor's front. Though not showing any overt damage to the tractor, the motor was still running and her father was nowhere in sight.

Mr. Levy trotted up to the tractor and turned it off. Cha Cha saw him swat at a hornet and noticing a swarm in the air, stayed back a considerable distance. She turned her attention to Mr. Levy who ran to a motionless figure on the ground.

"Mr. Vickery!" he shouted.

Cha Cha gasped. She could see only her father's overalls and work boots. Mr. Levy waved his straw hat through the air to discourage the buzzing swarm overhead. He cursed and slapped his arms as he made his way to the fallen man. Cha Cha moved to a different spot to see better while avoiding the hornets that patrolled the area. From her new vantage point, she observed the large papery nest on the ground close to the broken tree limb. The nest looked like a grotesque head of a deformed creature with two hollow black holes for eyes and a large dark hollow gap for the mouth where the hornets entered and exited. Chills ran through her and she stood frozen in place.

"Mr. Vickery!" Mr. Levy dragged her father's limp body a safe distance off, further from where Cha Cha stood. He fell to his knees, turned her father over onto his back, and moved his lifeless head from side to side. Even from a distance through the gray film of flying insects, she could tell her father's head did not move freely. Mr. Levy placed his fingertips on her father's neck, and after a moment of stillness, Mr. Levy hung his head in grief. He passed his fingers over her father's eyelids to close them. Cha Cha wanted to scream. She had not realized she had been holding her breath, but when she exhaled, her throat was so tight, she could not utter a sound.

Mr. Levy removed his light jacket and tucked it around his friend's head. Cha Cha watched the scene unfold as if it were someone else's father or a scene from a sad movie. Mr. Levy stood and turned, and their eyes met. Cha Cha bolted toward her house.

"Cha Cha! Wait!"

Cha Cha ran between the rows of trees and across the fields. When she reached her house, she saw her mother by the side door and without being seen, dashed around the opposite side.

Mr. Levy was not far behind. When he saw Mrs. Vickery, he ran toward her. Jolean walked out to meet him.

"Mr. Levy," Jolean said, "what is the matter?"

She waited impatiently as Mr. Levy caught his breath. Cha Cha peered around the corner of the house and listened as Mr. Levy explained the horrible news of her husband's demise.

"Are you sure he's… Well, I will phone the doctor and have him send an ambulance." Mr. Levy, would you please wait for their arrival? Did you see Charlise?"

"Yes, earlier, she was…trimming the rosemary. I'm so sorry, ma'am," he said between breaths. "Mrs. Vickery, I must go to him."

"Mr. Levy, you will need to stay until the emergency unit arrives. I do not know the layout of the gardens or the tree farm. I have never walked the fields. I thank you. My husband and Charlise have often told me what a wonderful neighbor you are."

"With all due respect, ma'am, I should go back. I can't leave him alone in the field. I can round up your daughter. She may be in the garden house."

Without further explanation, Jolean walked back into the house, letting the screen door close on its own.

Mr. Levy ran back and when he was a good way off, Cha Cha went to the garden house. She looked around at the bright yellow chairs, feeling weak in the legs. She sat and waited as her thoughts raced. None of them seemed to connect and tears fell down her face faster than she could wipe them away. After a time, she heard the sound of her father's tractor draw near, and for a brief moment, her heart leaped into the air. Maybe what she had seen was a mistake!

She held her hands over her closed eyes and prayed. "Dear God, if you will let my father be well and take the heavy burden from his heart, I promise never to whine about not having a happy home. The real blessing will be to have my father happy. God, can you hear me? You seem so far away." The tractor motor grated in her ears as it grew louder. She opened her eyes, ran outside, and saw Mr. Levy drive by on the tractor with her father's limp body draped across his lap. Stunned, and with her hopes crushed, she followed the tractor's wide tire tracks back to the house.

An ambulance pulled up the drive. Mr. Levy, who stood with a policeman, waved them over next to the tractor where Mr. Vickery's lifeless body was laid out on the ground. As Cha Cha approached, she saw one man check her father and then cover his face again with his jacket. He signaled another man and the two brought out a stretcher. Cha Cha felt her body grow heavy. Her heart raced, but her steps slowed. Mr. Levy turned as if he would now find Cha Cha at the garden house. Before he could take another step, he saw her.

"Cha Cha!" he called.

"Charlise!" her mother cried.

The words floated past her as if caught on the wind. Her knees gave out and she fell to the ground. Mr. Levy ran to her side.

"Cha Cha!" Mr. Levy got her on her feet and she stared at him blankly. "Are you okay?"

Cha Cha rubbed her eyes and tears burst forth.

Mr. Levy talked to her softly. "Your father had an accident. Your mother wants you to come home."

Cha Cha fell limply into his arms.

"This news is devastating." Mr. Levy explained to the police officer who joined him. "She was extremely close to her father. So was I." Mr. Levy's voice cracked and he wept. "Forgive me, he was a dear friend."

When consciousness returned, Cha Cha found herself being carried in the officer's arms. The stinging oils of rosemary and its sharp scent made her eyes burn. She welcomed the pain it gave her, rather than let the harsh reality of the unthinkable take its place.

Summoning all of her strength, she said, "My father is dead."

The officer put Cha Cha down. As soon as she was steady on her feet, she took off in a run through the maze of cornrows, and then collapsed once more into the warm, consoling earth. She opened her painful eyes, rolled onto her back, and looked skyward. She spoke to God, "I don't know you, but I sense you are there, all powerful. Or, are you a fake like Oz? Why, God? Why my father? Why this pain? I want my father! My sweet, lonely father. Why do you need him? I need him. Why couldn't you have helped him? He was a kind man with a sad heart." Cha Cha curled into a fetal position and cried into the earth.

The officer reached Cha Cha's side. She was inconsolable and incapable of walking, her grief was so great. Cha Cha allowed him to carry her once more across the fields to her house where Mr. Levy and her mother were waiting for their return.

Jolean said to her daughter, "Go wash yourself up and lie down."

"No, I want to be here with you, Mother."

The two stood in silence as they watched the doctor and emergency crew from a distance. The personnel returned with their conclusion—Mr. Vickery had died from hornet stings.

"My husband once had an allergic reaction from a bee string. He had been forewarned that he could die if it happened again." Jolean said these words in a matter-of-fact way, without despair.

Cha Cha was horrified. "Mother! Why didn't Father tell me?"

Mr. Levy spoke up. "Had I known, I would have moved that hornet's nest."

Jolean gave Cha Cha and Mr. Levy a disapproving look, as if the two were undermining her in front of the doctor. She excused herself and walked away toward the ambulance.

Cha Cha asked Mr. Levy if he would burn the hornets' nest.

"No child, your father would not want me to destroy it. He had a great respect for insects and their contribution to the planet. I will move it to a safer place. It is a mean, ugly looking thing."

Cha Cha moved closer to Mr. Levy and he put his arm around her. She looked up into her friend's face. "I can't allow my father to not be in the garden in the morning. Who will give me direction? How can he be dead?"

Mr. Levy spoke, "Cha Cha, my wife will come and stay with you and your mother. She is a great person. You will like having her close by."

"Yes, thank you. That will be so kind. Will you please ask Mother?"

Mr. Levy made sure Cha Cha was in the house when the time came for the ambulance to take her father away.

CHAPTER SEVEN

Saying Goodbye

The morning after her father's death, Cha Cha and her mother ate the breakfast Mrs. Levy prepared. Mrs. Levy took over the kitchen, which smelled of bacon, hot perking coffee, and sweet cinnamon buns. She left mother and daughter, and said she would return to check on them later.

Cha Cha ate every bite of the delicious meal. In a dream-like state, she savored the rare experience. How her father would have loved this morning meal. *Father*, she thought, *what will this world be like without you?* Cha Cha finished her meal in silence. After she excused herself, she went to the garden and threw up. Aimless in thought and with no chores slated for the day, she walked the corn-rows, kicking dirt clods as she went. Kind-hearted Mr. Levy had offered to greet any customers and give them the wretched news.

Her father was buried two days later at her mother's Baptist church. The casket was closed, and set on top was the picture of him in the frame Cha Cha had made, taken from his room.

The small church was packed with her father's customers paying their last respects. Cha Cha looked at their faces. She tugged on her mother's arm and whispered, "Mother, I am so proud all these people came to show how much they liked Father."

Her mother touched her two fingers to Cha Cha's lips for silence. Cha Cha felt surprised the gesture was gentle, almost loving. Cha Cha's heart leaped with a glimmer of hope. Perhaps now, her mother would turn to her for a closer relationship. She would have loved knowing her mother's feelings, but this was not to be. Though cordial, her mother had little to say after the service.

They left the cemetery after the men finished their job, and Mr. Levy drove Cha Cha and her mother home in Mr. Vickery's station wagon. Cha Cha felt tension well up inside her.

"Mother, may I open a window? I can't breathe."

"Mr. Levy, would you open your window?" her mother asked.

The air felt cool and fresh, and when she breathed it in, she started to cry. She bent forward and put her hands over her face. It was a deep, long outpouring, a pain no child should have to endure. Cha Cha kept her head down the rest of the drive home.

Upon arriving at the farm, her mother put her hand on Mr. Levy's shoulder. "I hope you will stay on at the farm. Thank you and Mrs. Levy for your kindness. Charlise and I will be fine. And could you please put my husband's station wagon away? We will take the bus if needed."

"I will take care of it."

Before he left, Cha Cha spoke up. "Mr. Levy, did you take care of the hornet's nest? I'd like to visit the spot." Mr. Levy, always respectful, looked to Jolean to see if she objected, but her expression was blank. "I want to place some of his favorite herbs and flowers there. And Mr. Levy, if it's not too much trouble, do you think you could build a bench for me and place it there?"

"Of course. Your father was my friend and a fine man, and I will miss him every day. Meet me at the garden house tomorrow morning."

Later, when she was on her own, Cha Cha walked the fields picking wildflowers and herbs to be placed on the ridge where her father died. As she walked, she was aware of her senses, yet nothing felt the same. She took off her shoes and pressed her feet into the

earth. The landscape looked exactly as it had the day before, the aromas coming off the herbs were the same, but it seemed as if a film had been laid over everything, dampening her experience. She left the flowers in Mason jars in front of the garden house.

The next morning, having slept well and feeling rested, Cha Cha ate breakfast alone, preferring not to rouse her mother. She went to meet Mr. Levy, and as the sound of his motor bike came within earshot, she felt a flutter of gaiety.

"Hi, Cha Cha." Mr. Levy saw the Mason jars full of flowers and attached them to the basket on the front of his bike. He knew her heart was broken, but tried to bring her a little lightness, no matter the circumstances. "Hop on, and hold onto me."

Even with the pain of her father's death, the thrill of riding on a motorbike was revitalizing. This time, the cool fresh air blew her hair and made her ears buzz in a pleasant way. She opened her mouth to feel the air enter her body.

When they reached the tree on the ridge top where her father's tractor had come to a stop, Cha Cha said, "Oh, thank you, Mr. Levy, that was wonderful! I think Father would have liked that you gave me a ride. The wind made all my worries disappear, at least for now."

She looked around. The broken branch was gone, as was the hornet's nest. Cha Cha laid herself down on the dirt and cried for her loss.

After a time, she wiped her eyes. "Mr. Levy, I will never be a child again."

"Such deep words, my dear. I don't believe that's true. A moment ago the wonder of childhood filled your eyes as you got off the bike. You'll see. That feeling may go to sleep, but it will always fight to jump out again."

As she suspected, her mother forbade her to ride on Mr. Levy's motorbike again. She never did, but Mr. Levy was right. She held that joyful experience in her heart, and often brought it to mind on a gloomy day.

True to his word, Mr. Levy made a bench and put it beneath the tree where Cha Cha could visit and reflect. She often placed flowers and other objects there, and had long talks with her father, the kind she could never get enough of when her father was alive.

The Levys were a godsend. Mrs. Levy brought in hot meals because Jolean stopped cooking. Cha Cha received the necessities. She was fed, clothed, and educated, but was not allowed to invite anyone to their home, which her mother continued to keep in pristine condition.

For the next two years, Cha Cha made good on her responsibilities to her mother, the tree farm, and her muffin business. In her few unstructured moments, she lived in the fantasy of her imagination.

When Cha Cha was thirteen, she received an invitation to a classmate's birthday party. She confided to Mr. Levy her longing to go, and feared her mother would refuse to let her.

"You must ask, child. Maybe I can help in some way," said Mr. Levy.

At supper, she worked up her nerve. "Mother, please, I promise to do extra chores and not ask annoying questions."

Her mother conceded when Mr. Levy stopped by the next day and volunteered to drive Cha Cha to the party. Cha Cha was ecstatic and thanked Mr. Levy over and over.

At the party, everyone sang "Happy Birthday" during the ritual lighting of the candles. Much ado was made over blowing out the candles and the girl's birthday wish, which was followed by cake and ice-cream. The girl opened a mountain of beautifully wrapped gifts and her mother threaded the ribbons and bows through her hair.

Everyone laughed and the lucky girl showed delight as she helped her guests roast marshmallows in the fireplace.

Cha Cha stood in the back, surprised to feel a smoldering jealousy at the fuss made over the birthday girl. She felt angry at her parents, including her father who loved her, yet never gave her so much as one lighted candle! She struggled with her envy, wondering if it was a sin for a person to be happy or to receive adoration to this extent. It didn't seem fair to see all the pretty, colorful new clothes when Cha Cha wore ugly homemade outfits to school that mimicked her mother's plain wardrobe. Why didn't her family show love the way this family did? She thought back to the happy families that came for Christmas trees. The cacophony of joyful party sounds in the room swirled around her. The room spun and Cha Cha felt ill. She sat down and held her head in her hands.

The birthday girl's mother rushed to Cha Cha's side. "Dear, are you all right?"

The honeyed concern in her voice made Cha Cha's stomach churn. She pleaded a headache, fled outside, and threw up outside Mr. Levy's waiting car. Mr. Levy went to her with a clean handkerchief and wiped her face. He put his arm around her shoulder and held the door as she got in.

Cha Cha was silent on the drive home until she could trust her voice wouldn't crack. "Thank you, Mr. Levy, for your kindness, for interceding with my mother, and for driving me to the party. And thank you for staying around. I couldn't have stood it much longer anyway."

He looked at her with sad eyes, knowing she needed more guidance than he would ever be able to give. "It's later than you think. What say we go home and have some tea?"

"Sorry, Mr. Levy. Maybe another day."

Mr. Levy chatted to cover Cha Cha's mood. He pulled into the drive and wished her a good night.

Cha Cha thanked him again and breathed in the cold night air. To her surprise, her mother had left the porch light on. He waited until she was at the door before he drove off.

Cha Cha's hand had no sooner touched the screen door when her mother's unwelcome voice came through the open window. "Charlise Charmaine, come in here right now!"

"Leave me alone!"

Her voice sounded as if it came from someone else. She had reached her limit, the horror of her life. Her insides ached. She was angry at her parents, the birthday girl, the Christmas tree customers, and God. Why didn't He hear her prayers? Her mother's demand swirled around her head, circling her ears like a vise. She hadn't planned to disobey, but her feet carried her into the rows of cedar trees where she collapsed. Her pent up tears poured out from her agony-filled young life. She felt out of control, unable to push back. Instead of release, the knot inside her tightened. Was this the kind of hurt her father felt being married to her mother? Why he secretly went to his liquor hiding place?

"Father," she cried, "you said there would be a rainbow for me!"

Bravely, she stood and brushed off the dirt from her plain, serviceable coat and walked back to the house with dread. Her footsteps on the wood planks of the porch squeaked, signaling her return. The porch light was still on. She half expected the door to be locked. It wasn't. *Might as well get it over with,* she thought as she walked the few steps to her mother's bedroom. Cha Cha tapped on the closed door.

"Charlise Charmaine." Her mother's soft words carried no anger or recrimination.

"Yes, Mother?" Cha Cha replied through the closed door. "May I come in?"

"No. You know how ill I am. You caused me enough worry today running off like that!"

Cha Cha slumped against the door and asked, "You worried about me?"

"Yes."

Holding onto hope, she asked, "Mother, may I have a cake with lighted candles on it?" In two days, she would turn fourteen.

CHAPTER EIGHT

An Enduring Heart

Her mother's lack of interest in life spread like spilled water. There was no resistance or reason for strength. Each day she faded a little more; the bloom on her cheeks disappeared and her hair lost its luster. She quit trying, even giving up Sunday Service at church.

Cha Cha was a dutiful daughter. At fourteen, when others her age were at gatherings with friends, football games, or going to parties, she became her mother's caregiver and head of the household. And when her mother stopped getting out of bed, Cha Cha came to her with checks to sign so their bills would be paid. Mrs. Levy would stop in on her mother and also helped Cha Cha with the shopping.

Studious by nature, Cha Cha's grades were near perfect. Even with her other responsibilities, she managed to finish school at fifteen years old, passing two grades ahead and graduating with highest honors. Mr. Levy came to her graduation in lieu of her mother.

"I am sure your father is proud of you," Mr. Levy said. "No one knows what the departed see. My wife tells me your mother is also proud of your accomplishments."

Wasting no time, Cha Cha continued her studies with mail-order college courses. Her studies siphoned off the energy that otherwise would have fueled despair. Each day, when her many chores were completed, she eagerly escaped into books.

Cha Cha continued to work the herb gardens and sell muffins on Saturdays. She found her father's black leather notebook, which contained all of his recipes for healing unguents and salves. His longtime customers still requested his products. It was too much work.

"Mother, I can't handle it all." Cha Cha sat in the small chair next to her mother's bed. Mr. Levy had already come on full-time, but it wasn't enough.

"Yes, Charlise. Our finances are such that we can afford to hire two new employees to assist him. Mr. Levy is a capable manager. I realize you have been carrying an enormous burden. Confer with Mr. Levy. He will know what to do. Now I'm tired." Her mother turned away, and Cha Cha left the room.

Her mother made sure Mr. Levy received a nice year-end bonus. Cha Cha was happy to give it to him. She liked to give the Levys little extras like baskets of assorted muffins and an occasional whimsical gift. Mr. Levy was indispensable. Cha Cha trusted him. He took care to stay after the house and outbuildings to keep them from deteriorating. Most of all, he was Cha Cha's one true friend, and for that, she was grateful.

At Christmastime, Mr. Levy decorated a large tree in front of the house. The evening he was to light it up, he told Cha Cha, "Leave the shutters open in your mother's room so she will be able to see it."

"We have never had a tree lit or celebrated Christmas. Mother will be upset."

"No, my dear, I don't believe she will. In my heart I believe there are secrets your mother carries. We will never know what pain or joy she feels alone in her room. Let's give her this piece of magic." He turned the lights on.

Cha Cha's eyes grew misty at the sight and she gave Mr. Levy a hug. "Thank you for this gift." A part of her wanted to share the moment with her mother, but she decided not to risk losing her wonderful feelings. "Mr. Levy, did you know my father well?"

"No, but I did consider him a good friend."

"I ask because I want to know why he sold trees yet we never had one."

Mr. Levy took Cha Cha's hand, "Look! There is a light on in your mother's room. She sees the tree. It's okay."

Cha Cha's life continued to consist of work, home, caretaking, the muffin and herb business, and her studies. She missed her father's company every day, but she never had another episode where she lost control. She simply focused her energy elsewhere. The atmosphere in the house was melancholy. Years passed without much notice and her daily routines remained consistent. To ease her exhaustion, she hired a local woman to help care for her mother and provide light housework. Cha Cha, now eighteen, told Mr. Levy, "I feel eighty."

Cha Cha took a taxi into town for the weekly household shopping, a fact known to Mr. Levy. He offered to give her a ride, but she thanked him and said, "My mother has forbidden me to accept rides, even with you, Mr. Levy."

"Cha Cha, you're an adult now and there's no reason you can't be more independent. I can teach you how to drive your father's old station wagon. It's been sitting in the barn all these years and I'm sure it needs a lot of work—new hoses and belts, not to mention tires, a battery, and who knows what else? It would still be cheaper than buying a new car and you need to get around on your own."

Cha Cha listened. She liked to believe her father would have said the same thing.

Mr. Levy continued. "The owner of a service station is a friend of mine. I can have him take a look at it. What do you say?"

Cha Cha looked at Mr. Levy's kind face. Her chest felt expansive and she felt a fluttering inside, as if her heart was taking flight. Of course! The car would make her life easier and clear up her busy schedule. She felt enlivened. "Why, thank you! Yes! Let's do it."

"Great! I'll arrange to have it towed. After it's been properly serviced, we can work in some driving lessons."

"Father's car keys are in the house," Cha Cha said. "Funny, isn't it, how I see them almost every day, and I never thought to learn how to drive. I'll leave them for you on the car seat. Oh, and I'll pay for the repairs out of my own savings. You are such a good friend. For now, let's keep this between us. I'll tell my mother when the time is right."

Mr. Levy nodded. He stuck his thumbs under his overall straps and Cha Cha could see he felt pleased. She hurried on homeward and silently rejoiced. *Today, my life changed. Maybe this is a sign—I am ready for the next chapter in life. Mr. Levy is going to help me gain some freedom. I can endure.*

There was no way to enter the house unknown as the creaking porch gave away her arrival. Her mother called out as Cha Cha opened the door, "Charlise Charmaine! Do try to prepare my meal on time. If only I could do it myself." Being bedridden had not weakened her mother's voice, but today, she didn't care; a hopeful light shone in her heart.

Cha Cha had tried to turn around her mother's ill humor and heartache, serving special muffins created to soothe and lift her mood, but there was no undoing her mother's choice. Though she struggled at times, Cha Cha would not allow herself to become bitter or fall into self-pity. She found it helpful to limit time with her mother. When the muffins didn't work, she lightly spiked her mother's nightly tea with a sleeping potion. No longer awakened by her mother's imaginary requirements, both of them were assured a good night's rest. It surely did her mother no harm, and did Cha Cha a world of good.

Cha Cha couldn't wait for her father's car to be finished. She named the peach-colored station wagon "Woody" after the refurbished wooden sides. In no time she learned to drive. Mr. Levy provided a parking place beside his garage away from the main house, shielding Cha Cha from her mother's control. She rewarded herself with stolen adventures into the outside world. Her clandestine endeavors made her newfound freedom all the sweeter. She discovered roadside flea markets and became a wise shopper, discreetly saving on her bargain finds. She longed to surprise her mother with a special item, but unlike the Levys who appreciated her gifts, she was sure her mother would ask probing questions. Still, she imagined wrapping up something and leaving it on her dinner tray.

Cha Cha found delight in purchasing her own personal items. She fell in love with semi-precious jewelry. The colorful stones made her feel pretty. Each morning, she selected a necklace and admired it in the mirror. "Charlise Charmaine," she said to herself, you are worthy of the happiness this brings." She tucked her necklace inside her blouse where her mother wouldn't see it.

At times, she felt her father watched over her. As she sat on the bench Mr. Levy made, a red-tailed hawk would soar overhead, lighting high on a tall pine and making her wonder about what was on the other side. Her father had connected with the natural world and passed that knowledge along to her. Would he choose to be that lone blue jay picking off an insect on the rosemary bloom? In any case, his words on the wind filled her heart, "Yes, my beautiful Cha Cha, happiness awaits you. I've seen it. You will be blessed."

CHAPTER NINE

Letting Go

As Cha Cha grew stronger, her mother grew weaker. For too long, the mournful Mrs. Jolean Vickery rebuffed her daughter's valiant attempts to coax her out of bed. What started as a peevish act of willful temper, developed into a full-blown biological condition as her muscles atrophied and her complaints were no longer imaginary.

Cha Cha continued to leave notes under her mother's pillow, tucking them in when her mother was up tending to her personal needs. She wrote about her gratitude for the Levy family's support, how the cedar seedlings had grown, visiting birds, and the budding jonquils ready to burst forth with yellow gold. Spring would soon be joining them. As a test to confirm whether her mother read the notes, she wrote about Woody. Surely she would acknowledge that bit of information. Cha Cha prepared herself for her mother's fury, but the revelation proved otherwise. "Charlise," her mother said, "when you take out your father's wagon, pick up some strawberry ice cream."

Cha Cha's jaunts into town and the countryside became the core of her life. As she took in the sights, she believed there was a place for her somewhere. Days passed into years. One day, while working in the garden with Mr. Levy, she realized his hair had turned grey. His kind face sported wrinkles, and he seemed shorter than he used to be.

"How is it seventeen years have passed since my father died?"

Mr. Levy pulled off his work gloves. Resting on his hoe, he said, "What a shame your father's accident left you to take care of your mother and the farm when you were so young."

"I never could have come through it without your friendship and guidance."

"Listen to me. When your mother passes, sell this house and hit the road. There's a beautiful world out there. Meet people. Your time for adventure is just around the corner."

The day came at last when her mother let go. Cha Cha set down the breakfast tray and gazed at her mother, relieved she had died peacefully in her sleep. Cha Cha took the note her mother held, and without looking at it, placed it in an open box with the others Cha Cha had written over the years.

"Mother, why couldn't you tell me? We both missed so much; now it's too late." Cha Cha bent down on her knees and taking her mother's soft, cold hand said, "I forgive you."

Cha Cha dealt with the coroner and the funeral home, dry-eyed. Now she knew her mother had loved her. All those unfruitful years! She was unable to make a meaningful connection, one that would improve their daily lives, but with no regrets for trying, she felt liberated.

Cha Cha dressed in black and put on her favorite red stone necklace. The garnet sparkled. She would not need to tuck it out of sight ever again. Standing in front of a full-length mirror, she looked at herself. "I am a thirty-two-year-old woman. I can take flight." She took in a deep breath and felt tension melt away.

Was Mr. Levy right? Was she free? She walked to the open window overlooking the garden. "Father, how will I know which way to go?" She closed her eyes and opened her heart in search of an answer.

From deep within she heard her father's voice, "Cha Cha, see what's in front of you. Do not turn away and you will make the right decision."

Cha Cha buried her mother next to her father after a short, sparsely attended service. Mrs. Levy left while Cha Cha watched two men shovel the last bit of dirt onto her mother's grave.

"Are you okay?" Mr. Levy asked.

"Yes. There's something I need to do. Thank you, though. I appreciate your concern."

Mr. Levy squeezed her around the shoulders and caught up to his wife. Cha Cha picked up a bag of bulbs and her father's old trowel. She planted jonquil bulbs, then replanted the blooming plants the men unearthed while digging the grave. For a brief moment, her mind went back to a rare show of affection she'd shared with her mother. It happened at one of the saddest times in Cha Cha's life—her father's burial.

Together, Cha Cha and her mother planted dozens of jonquil bulbs around her father's plot. In fact, it was the only time Cha Cha saw her mother work the earth and she was surprised at her ability. They planted in silence. When the bulbs were in the earth, her mother squeezed Cha Cha's dirt encrusted hand. She wanted to hug her Mother and let her know how much the small gesture meant. Instead she wept for her dismal life and her father, who lay below and for her sad mother standing beside her.

In her innocent child's voice, she said, "Mother, did you and Father ever love each other?"

"Yes, in our own way. But it is private matter between me and your father."

Cha Cha said goodbye to her mother and father. She picked up her tools and drove out of the cemetery with a feeling she couldn't identify.

Woody's steady engine sounded comforting to her ears. She cranked down the windows. The wind caressed her face, which was once more wet with tears—from grief or a chance at a new life, she was not sure. For the first time she had no one to answer to but herself. She opened her thoughts, removing all boundaries, and tasted the sweetness of true freedom.

"Yes! Yes! I will meet new people and enjoy a good talk with a neighbor. I'll say, 'And how are you, Mrs. Smith? Isn't it a beautiful day? Say hello to your family. Well, I must be off—I've a million things to do. See you at the town social!'"

Cha Cha laughed at her silliness, but took delight in the sound of the words. She let her mind soar—ideas, dreams, visions of what a life could be—her life. She stored these in her heart. Eager to begin, she pressed a little harder on the accelerator.

When she arrived back at the house, her mother's attorney, Mr. Redman, was waiting for her on the porch, holding a packet of papers. He expressed his condolences.

"Thank you. I assume you are here about my mother's Will. I'd like a little time. Can this wait a few days?"

"I beg your pardon, Miss Vickery. I meant no disrespect. It should come as no surprise that your mother left everything to you, but that's not why I'm here. However, I can wait until I hear from you. Again, my condolences."

It was a warm, early spring day. Cha Cha walked into the house as if she would not be met by silence. She raised the shades, opened windows, and walked through the house without concern for the sound her heels made on the wood floors. She examined her mother's fine antiques—now hers—with a new appreciation for their beauty. She went to the side porch, took off her shoes, and walked out among the Christmas trees. Her feet pressed into the soil. As a child, she longed to run barefoot, but her mother forbade it.

"Charlise," she could hear her mother say, "you are not going to look like a street urchin. Put your shoes on, now!"

A surge of defiance called her back to the house. She grabbed her car keys, drove to the store, and bought herself a six-pack of beer. As soon as she returned home, she opened a beer. For a brief second, she felt wicked—a term her mother had used to describe alcohol, which had never been allowed in the house. This was a new day and a new life.

"Here's to me!" The cool liquid went down her throat. "Unshackled! This is my Independence Day!"

The taste was new and refreshing. It cleared her palate and she understood why characters on TV would have a good time at a back-yard party with a beer in one hand and a freshly grilled hamburger in the other. As she continued to drink, she felt different. She caught a glimpse of her reflection in the kitchen window and asked, "Who are you?" Feeling giddy, she lifted her beer. "We will have many adventures in seeking the answer to that question." She finished the brew and opened another.

Thinking ahead, Cha Cha looked around the house. What items held meaning for her? She took a mental inventory and then wandered over to the garden house. There, she did the same thing, eyeing the Tibetan bells hanging on the door, tools she and her father had both used over the years in the garden and for making his healing salves. It was time to let go, but there were some things she wanted to bring with her into her next life. She felt ready to meet her next adventure, a life of unknown possibilities.

Curious, she returned to the house and phoned the attorney with whom she had met and sent away hours earlier. At first, Mr. Redman danced around his intentions before declaring his interest in her house and farm. Would she consider selling? Mr. Levy was right. Her adventure had moved up from being around the corner to being right at her feet.

Cha Cha made arrangements to sell the house and most of its contents, as well as the Christmas tree farm to Mr. Redman, who said he and his family had many fond memories buying trees and produce over the years. He and his grown son would take over, but he promised to employ Mr. Levy, not only because Mr. Levy still loved the farm, but because he was every bit as valuable an asset as the land itself. Mr. Redman felt there was something magical about the trees, and he hoped to transition into a new career with his family's support. For him, it was a childhood dream come true.

Cha Cha could now focus on the practical. Soon she would leave and another family would take over. She hoped they would bring the long-sought happiness the house had missed during the time she had lived there. The process of packing became part of the adventure and she started to set items aside. There were legal papers and the cash her father had insisted on keeping in the house. She folded her clothes and her beautiful gemstone jewelry. In the outbuildings, her father's mortar and pestle caught her eye. She picked them up with reverence, along with his leather notebook filled with healing recipes. She lifted the Tibetan prayer bells from the door and imagined putting them elsewhere—a new place she would call home. Inside the greenhouse, she took a couple of evergreen seedlings, herb seeds, and a basket of tools. She couldn't bear to leave her father's hoe and shovel; she'd seen him use them a thousand times. And she couldn't forget his framed picture.

Once more, she entered the quiet of the house. She picked up the framed picture and set it with her things. For a moment, she thought to take the box of saved notes she had written, before remembering she had buried them with her mother. She walked through each room, looking around at her mother's things—the weekly-polished silverware, the fancy, unused china in the ornate cabinet, the soft-scrubbed floorboards, and vowed never to spend countless hours on what had come to nothing.

On impulse, Cha Cha scooped up her mother's prized sterling silver and put it in a grocery sack. She set aside an extra cash bonus for Mr. Levy, placed it on top and taped the bag closed. The humble wrappings of her gift concealed what she was certain would be a delightful surprise. She had already given several pieces of antique furniture to the Levy family. She would have given it all to them, had they wanted it. She would miss Mr. Levy, but at least she could write him when she found a place to settle.

Getting back to her business at hand, she remembered her father's old camp stove, a sleeping bag, and a few odds and ends. She packed up Woody's interior. With a bit of space left over, she decided to add a bit of serendipity by taking items without reason, believing there would come a time and place when it would go to someone in need of that very thing. She worked throughout the night until even the storage box on Woody's roof rack was filled to capacity.

Now, after weeks of preparation, everything was done. She sat on her porch for the last time. Cha Cha closed her eyes, listened to the familiar sounds of crickets, and inhaled the cedar's fresh smell. A lone night bird sang its song, and a far-off hound barked at a night movement. An owl hooted and was answered by another farther away. Rather than pulling her into her old environment, the sounds released her. She felt woozy, went inside the house, and slept her last night, fully dressed on the sofa.

She awoke with a start to the slam of a car door. The first fingers of light streamed across her face. She sat up and looked outside. Her skin tingled in the cool morning air. She waved to Mr. Levy as he went to work, like any other day. She made coffee and started her last batch of muffins to take on the road.

Mr. Redman walked up the steps and called inside. She greeted him. The two finished their business over coffee. How different this was from the days when she cowered from her mother's wrath in the same kitchen. Mr. Redman thanked her and took the house keys. He told her to stay as long as she needed to, and then he excused himself.

Cha Cha recognized her time had come. She packed up her few last items, leaving a few muffins for the Redmans. Spreading a state road map on the kitchen table, she closed her eyes, took a deep breath and slowly moved her index finger, guided as if it were on an Ouija board. Her finger stopped on Divine, Georgia.

She dashed off a letter to the Levy's thanking them for their many kindnesses throughout the years and added it to their gift. She ran next door, said her goodbyes to Mrs. Levy and left her the package. She ran back and found Mr. Levy tending to the seedlings. She hugged him, knowing it would probably be for the last time.

"I am so grateful to you and for everything you have done for me," she said. "You made a difference in my life, and I hope I can take what I've learned and pass it along. You've been a treasured friend and I'll never forget you."

Mr. Levy started to say something, but instead he bit his lip and his eyes became wet. "Be sure to write us."

Cha Cha bounded out. "Goodbye trees! Goodbye herbs!" She half ran to her car. "Goodbye house," she said gently. She felt called to walk up the porch steps one more time. She pressed her hand on the door. "Blessings to you. May you become the home you were meant to be with the Redmans." *Red,* she thought, *the first color of the rainbow.*

Now that she had said goodbye to her old life, she thought, *I feel different. I'm not Cha Cha anymore. I'm certainly not Charlise or Charmaine. I feel like Cha now. Yes, Cha!* She felt a subtle shift as she acknowledged her new identity, lighter, yet full of energy, and unshakable in her commitment to move on. Cha knew her happiness was up to her and not something external. "Remember," Mr. Levy had once said, "happiness lies within a person."

Cha walked around the car. Satisfied with its condition, she got in. Taking up her father's black leather notepad, she noted the date and time, the miles on the car and a brief note about new beginnings. Without a doubt, the enormity of this day was pivotal to her life. She turned the key and thrilled as the engine purred to life.

She pulled out of the drive, and seeing the mailbox, she stopped and got out. She approached the mailbox with its rainbow paint faded from years of weathering, and went to work. She felt her father's love all around her.

With the mailbox stuffed into the back of the wagon, she pulled onto the road. She cracked down the window and shouted, "It's my turn! Divine, Georgia, my heart is open. I am on my way!"

"It's all about being lost enough to want to find yourself."

—Robert Frost

CHAPTER TEN

Rest Stops

Rolling down an unfamiliar highway on a real journey was new to her, as were the feelings quickening her body. The classic station wagon was timeworn, though completely restored. Mr. Levy had overseen the work. Smiling, she thought of what Mr. Levy said when he picked up Woody.

"It was a bit difficult to get your car back. Those fellows at the station almost fought each other to work on her. She is a beauty. They don't make them like this anymore."

Cha loved the feel of Woody's power on the small of her back whenever she accelerated. She drove along with the window open, enjoying the different elements the breezes carried—freshly mown grass, sweet mists of soft rain, and the scent of honeysuckle mixed with wildflowers. Now and then she passed a newly plowed field. The earthy scent of rich soil stirred her soul.

When a small, green grasshopper hitched a ride on the front window, she pulled to the side of the road, carefully plucked it off, and placed it on a roadside wildflower. *Can I take in all of life? How much better can it get?* She wondered about her chosen destination. What would it be like? How would she fit in? There was no way of knowing what would await her: conflict, adventure, goodwill from the citizens of Divine, and dare she imagine romance? Now that she was in control, she placed her focus on being happy.

Cha covered about one hundred fifty miles the

first day, at times veering from the highway in favor of small connecting roads. She drove small town main streets and stopped at parks to stretch her legs. No matter what turn her life would take, the trip to Divine would be etched in her memory forever.

In late afternoon, she pulled into an old Shell station. She was tired, and the wagon needed a fill-up. The owner gassed up the wagon and cleaned her windshield.

Admiring her ride, he said, "This old gal looks almost new. Where you headed?"

"Divine, Georgia."

"Can't say I've ever heard of it. Pull the hood latch." He checked the oil. "Wouldn't want you to get stranded somewhere out there."

Cha yawned so big her eyes watered. "Excuse me! I'm not used to driving all day."

"Well, if you want to park here and rest, you're welcome. I've got sodas and snacks inside. Restroom is around the corner. Picnic table is over yonder. By the way, my name is Billy."

"I'd like that very much, thanks. I'm Cha." She parked Woody and went inside where she picked out a few treats and paid for gas.

A small, barefoot girl came in and clung to Billy's side. Cha smiled at her.

He looked down at his daughter and said, "My wife passed some months back. I'm doing what I can, but Annie's grieving hard. She hardly says a peep. Sometimes I feel like I've lost them both."

Cha understood the little girl's sadness. The desperation on Billy's face told of his wish for his child's healing. Cha felt the need to help both of them find peace and hope for the tomorrows to come while honoring the memory of their loved one.

"I feel for you," Cha said, "as I have also experienced loss. If you'll allow me, I have just the thing. I need a few minutes to wash up, but then I'll make tea for us. I have some great-tasting homemade muffins I would like to share. Will you join me?"

Cha prepared the tea on her portable campfire stove and opened a box of muffins. *Look at me,* she thought, *I've invited new friends for tea, and they said "Yes!"* She thought of the odd items she packed at the last minute, remembering her angel wings saved from a role in a grade school play. She had been so proud of the beautiful green, glitter-dusted wings. Her father had attached them to her bedroom wall where they served as fanciful art until she removed them mere hours ago.

Billy and the silent little girl came over to the picnic table where their tea and snacks waited. Cha presented the wings with a flourish, and said, "Dear, beautiful one, when you find yourself missing your beloved mother, put on these angel wings and know your mother is looking down on you from heaven. She'll see how much you love and miss her, and she will be happy knowing you are happy."

Cha helped Annie into the straps that held the wings in place. The little girl's face lit up.

"Daddy, look!" Annie exclaimed, spinning around to show him the wings. Billy gathered his daughter into his arms, wings and all.

"Daddy, do you think Mommy's wings are green?"

"I don't know, but I am sure she picked a wonderful color. Maybe she picked butterfly wings; she loved butterflies."

"Oh, Daddy! Mommy with butterfly wings—like mine!"

Billy smiled and tipped his teacup toward Cha. She could tell he felt emotional hearing his child's laughter.

Throughout their teatime, complete with Cha's lemon blueberry muffins, the little girl was a chatterbox. Billy laughed as his child danced circles around the picnic table, making her wings move. He picked her up as they took their leave, and said, "Cha, you have been a godsend. Thank you. You will be safe here. Rest well, and we will see you in the morning. It's going to be a star-filled night."

Though sleepy, Cha lay on the picnic table and

drew inspiration from the starry sky. She thought of the times she had secretly opened her bedroom window, stuck her head out and gazed at the stars she loved so much. Now she could stargaze every night if she chose to. *One day*, she mused, *my rainbow's end will take me to the Milky Way with my husband and child. There will be a perfect sky, and we will enjoy it together in all of its beauty.* Placing her hand over her heart, she wept at nature's beauty and the peace she felt when a shooting star whizzed across the sky, sealing her good fortune.

As Cha laid out her sleeping bag across the seat in the station wagon, she decided she'd had a very good first day. She trusted her intuition when packing and it had bolstered her faith in herself and in her journey. She said a silent prayer for her continued safe travel along the road to Divine.

Before succumbing to sleep, Cha recorded her day in her notebook, expressing gratitude. She wrote about the beautiful view of the stars, and special moments while on her drive, simple pleasures like waving to strangers as they picked up their mail from roadside mailboxes.

The next morning, Cha woke refreshed. She used the station facilities, and lit the camp stove for tea. An unearthly sound startled her. She heard it again—a mule, perhaps? It seemed the animal was in distress. She looked across the nearby fields to find the source of the noise, but saw nothing.

Just then, Billy and Annie pulled up to open the gas station. The little girl jumped out of the truck and ran to Cha, her angel wings floating behind her. She said, "Miss Cha, my daddy and I got a sack of egg and cheese biscuits. Will you have breakfast with us? I got a new kitten last night and I want to name it Chachie after you. Is that okay?"

"Yes! How sweet." Cha smiled.

Billy joined them. "Annie loves her wings."

As they breakfasted, the screeching returned. "Billy, what is that sorrowful noise?"

"Instead of paying his bill, a man abandoned a donkey and his trailer on my lot last week with a note telling me what a nasty-tempered creature she was. No one can get near her—she bites and kicks, and to top it all, she has a skin problem. I've been asking around, but I can't sell her. Heck, I can't give her away! Her name is Ariabella. The note said she was once a good animal. You wouldn't know it now. I reckon I need to move her so she can get some fresh grass."

"She sounds miserable, poor thing." Cha took out one of her special muffins and followed Billy and Annie to the back of the gas station where the donkey was tied to a tree.

Cha took measured steps toward the scared animal. Its long ears went back, and she saw the fear and distrust in the animal's eyes. As she neared, she sensed a glimmer of hope as the little donkey leaned forward in curiosity.

The donkey perked her ears as Cha spoke in the soft tones her father had used. The donkey wagged her ears from back to front as it considered the unfamiliar person before her. The animal started to relax, seeming to find Cha agreeable.

Slowly extending a muffin out before her as an offering, Cha approached the donkey. "Hello, Ariabella. What a pretty name. Good girl."

Ariabella stamped one of her feet and shook, sending sparkling dust particles into the air. Lulled by the scent of food and Cha's crooning, the donkey's nose slowly moved closer to the muffin on the flat of her hand. While Ariabella sniffed the muffin, she kept her gaze on Cha's eyes. Two wounded souls connected. Ariabella flapped her muzzle over the muffin, trusting, yet cautious as she nibbled a few morsels.

Billy chuckled, "Well, now, looks like you two get along or that muffin's pure magic. You can have her and the trailer."

Having never been around animals, she mulled over the responsibility before her. The donkey's wounds needed treatment. Ariabella's situation tore at Cha's heart.

She moved closer to the donkey, and said, "Ariabella, do you want to go with me? I am on a journey and it's possible we will be a great comfort to each other. I've never had so much as a pet, but I have a lot of love to give." The donkey moved closer and nudged Cha with her nose. Cha said, "I will take that as a sign." She stroked her hand along the donkey's neck and the touch was received without fear, as if the donkey was waiting for the right person to rescue her.

"Your wagon can take the load, but you'll need a hitch. My brother will be here soon to mind the store, and then I can scoot back home for a few things. You don't mind waiting, do you? There's a flea market across the road that might catch your fancy."

"I'll be back." Cha gave Ariabella one final stroke on her scarred nose. Ariabella snorted as Cha walked off.

The morning sky was ocean blue with fluffy white clouds. A few cars passed along the narrow road in front of the gas station. Across the road behind a fence with an open gate, she saw the flea market. Several cars had pulled in front. The area was slowly coming to life.

Opening the car door, Cha took out her handbag and found an amethyst necklace to wear. She felt better when she wore jewelry. She handed her car keys to Billy and crossed the road in search of treasures.

The first array of items she spotted included a string of vivid purple pom-poms—the perfect thing to add pizzazz to a sickly, sad donkey. At the next table, she purchased a yellow stuffed dinosaur and a small hand-painted dish decorated with a beach scene. On impulse, she bought a new-in-the-box coffee urn. She strolled through the market and stopped before a plate of assorted fruit pies too irresistible to pass up, which she bought to share with Annie, Billy, and Billy's brother.

After getting permission to use the hose behind the station, Cha decided to wash Ariabella, believing the animal would appreciate the care. Though no longer scrappy, she would feel better once she had been bathed. Then Cha could apply her healing salve to the donkey's sores. The process would help her gain the animal's trust.

As Cha gave Ariabella a bath, Annie watched, wide-eyed, while munching on a peach pie. The donkey startled and brayed a few times, but allowed the cold water wash with herbal shampoo. Cha alternately laughed and comforted as she cleaned the donkey from head to tail. Ariabella visibly relaxed when the healing salve was applied.

As Ariabella's coat dried in the sun, Cha and Annie watched Billy weld the trailer hitch in place. Annie explained to Cha that her daddy wore his hat turned beneath his welder's hood so sparks wouldn't fly down his shirt.

When he was through, they took time to chat. Billy explained he was also a beekeeper. He told her stories of bees that had taken up residence where they didn't belong and how he transferred them to an empty hive. "More honey for us all," he told Cha with a big, assuring smile. She felt as though they could talk all day, but the wagon stood at the ready.

Billy would not allow Cha to pay him for the trailer hitch. He showed her how to hitch the trailer to the wagon, and then they retrieved Ariabella. The donkey had been transformed. She sported a shiny, spiked mane and a clean coat smelling of herbs. She wore her own "necklace" of regal purple, fluffy pom-poms. They loaded in handfuls of alfalfa and walked the donkey into the trailer without incident. She was a changed animal, as if she knew she would never be mistreated again.

Billy and Annie presented Cha with jars of honey. Cha hugged Annie and thanked Billy for his kindness. She wished them blessings and took her leave with a song in her heart.

The road to Divine stretched before her and even with the extra weight of the trailer, Woody proved her mettle. Cha felt optimistic about the future. Her troubled past was on the mend, and she could scarcely wait to see what the next day would bring.

CHAPTER ELEVEN

Divine Beginnings

Cha quickly adjusted to the feel of the trailer hitched to the rear bumper of the station wagon. Billy had set a precedent for her journey. He had shown kindness and compassion by extending himself to help a stranger. She thought of her dear friend, Mr. Levy, and his kind heart. These were the qualities she hoped to share with others.

She remembered being on her first outing alone after Mr. Levy had taught her how to drive. The air that day was exhilarating, crisp and cool, with orange and gold autumn leaves flying through the air. She felt intoxicated, and wanted it to go on forever. She completed her shopping and was loading bags of groceries into the car when she noticed an attractive pair of white majorette boots with green tassels sitting on the ground next to her wagon. There were no other cars or people near her.

"God? Has an angel on your cheering team dropped these to Earth?" She picked up the boots, and *glory hallelujah*, they were her size! She smiled all the way home, and at the last second, turned into

Mr. Levy's driveway, bursting with hysterical laughter. She'd roared until her sides hurt. Had she ever laughed so hard? It felt so good.

It dawned on her there were moments of joy to be found and others she could create. She felt as if she had been given a rare jewel. Imagine that! You could make your own pleasure!

She hid the boots from her mother. Such deceptive measures had become a matter of course. After she put away the groceries, she closed the bedroom door behind her and imagined how the boots would look with this dress or those pants. Taking off all her clothes, she checked out her body. She imagined her long, white, freckled legs as tan as a movie star's. At eighteen, her tall frame was beautifully proportioned. She put on her boots and pulled a short slip over her head. She admired herself in the mirror. *Wow! Is that really me?* She tucked her boots in the back of her closet behind her long wool coat, and when she looked at them, it reminded her she could capture bits of glee. The white majorette boots held special meaning. She couldn't leave them behind, and so she packed them in the antique trunk along with other treasures and placed them in the woody.

At her next stop on the road to Divine, a general store, Cha would have donned the boots if they had been easy to get to. She felt she could bring joy by being friendly and relying on her intuition to make the right purchases for future gifts. She found a supply of pretty yellow boxes that looked like they would hold a batch of muffins, along with a roll of purple ribbon. While she wasn't about to go back to present them to Billy and Annie, she had a feeling she would use them soon. She wrote down the store's name and phone number. She liked to imagine how her finds would help her leave a trail of smiles and delightful surprises. She didn't know how she developed a knack for giving the perfect gift for others' needs, but she recognized it as one

of her gifts to the world. This must have been an example of what her father meant when he told her she had talents others did not.

Ariabella had been quiet during the ride, but when Cha spotted a feed store, she decided to stop. The folks there let the donkey wander through a fenced yard for some exercise. The sight of her frolicking about with her purple pom-poms dancing around her neck brought cheer to those who saw her. It turned out that Ariabella was a bit of a ham, showing off for any audience. Cha considered their recommendations on what to feed her, and they loaded hay into the trailer.

As a token of her appreciation, she wasted no time making a gift of muffins. She placed them in the bright, sunny-yellow boxes and tied them with purple ribbon. As an afterthought, she tucked in an herb sprig and presented it to the workers at the feed store. She wished them well and more, that their dreams would come true. She knew dreams came true; she was living hers.

On the final leg of her trip, she bounced around entrepreneurial ideas for a unique muffin shop. She imagined an ideal set up, a two-story building where she could live and work. That would be another dream come true.

It was late afternoon when she spotted the sign preceding the town. "Divine," she said. "Ariabella, we're here!"

She rounded a scenic curve and took in the charming homes dotting the edge of the village. The road was lined with dogwoods, and white petals blew like snow on the breeze. The sight was enchanting.

She crossed a charming stone bridge with a flowing stream below. Cha pulled onto the side of the road, gravel crunching beneath her tires. Smooth pebbles lined the banks of the stream, reminding her of the creek she loved to visit as a child. The village shops were up ahead on the right side of the road, and a small post office faced opposite.

She got out of Woody to check on Ariabella. She

lifted the shuttered side window of the trailer and hooked it open. Ariabella felt more secure this way and was less likely to bray when Cha walked out of sight.

Cha figured she would give the small village a look-see, maybe drop into the local eatery and ask some resident about renting a store. The first building wasn't a building at all, but an old railway car that had been remodeled into a diner. When Cha opened the door to the diner, she saw a few patrons, including a man wearing a sheriff's uniform.

Before she could say anything, he asked, "New in town?"

She guessed he would know. "I just arrived to build a new life. I'm interested in opening a business here. Would you know of any storefronts that would be suitable for a muffin shop, preferably something with a small living area?"

"Sure do. You'll want to meet that man sitting on the end of the counter."

He gestured and Cha followed his gaze to a man who took her breath away.

CHAPTER TWELVE

Just Might Be

T he tall, good-looking man caught her eye. He was rugged,
a little scruffy, and sported a trim beard. He wore a carpen-
ter's belt around his waist and, as she approached, she de-
tected the smell of fresh-cut wood. He exuded masculinity. Kindness
shone in his aquamarine eyes, which crinkled at the corners as he
smiled at her.

"So, you're here to build a new life?" he remarked in a friendly,
husky voice.

Remembering her manners, Cha blinked several times
to keep from staring. "Yes." She realized she was flirting and
felt her face flush. It was all so new. "I'm getting a fresh
start. A store, and…" She felt flustered and tried to recov-
er. "Pastureland, close by. I have a four-legged companion to consider."

"A dog?"

"No," Cha replied. "A donkey." He laughed
and her cheeks burned. "Her name is
Ariabella."

"I'm Rob Brodie."

"I'm Cha."

They shook. His big hand was callused and
his grip strong.

"I'd like to meet Ariabella. Then we can talk."

"I'm parked over there, that peach-colored woody with the at-tached trailer."

She released his hand and missed its warmth. He laid a few dollars on the counter, got up, and held the diner door for her. He was taller than Cha, well over six feet, and he bent his head to miss the top of the doorway. Cha felt light-headed in a good way as she walked to the trailer.

Ariabella was restless and wanted out. Cha talked to her, rubbing her neck and head to keep her calm, and if she were to be truthful, to calm herself.

Rob didn't wait to be introduced. He walked over and the don-key stretched out her neck. Rob scratched her around the ears, and said, "Hello, beautiful."

Aria bobbed her head and nudged forward.

"Now I've made two new friends," he said.

Wow! Cha thought. *I can't believe I'm actually having a conver-sation with a handsome man, and he called me "friend." Life is looking good!*

"Cha, look down the street." Rob leaned in close. "That fourth little cottage has potential. A muffin shop, you say?" Cha nodded. "That used to be a sandwich shop. The apartment is upstairs. In the back, there's a fenced-in lot that extends to the property next to it—all vacant, at the moment, and available for rent or purchase. Oh, and a shed for your pal."

Cha hardly knew what to say. It sounded perfect, as if she had been showered with a heavenly miracle granting her heart's desire. "Unbelievable," she breathed.

"Would you like to see it now?"

"May I bring Ariabella and let her walk around the land?"

Rob nodded with a smile. Cha clipped the donkey's rope to her halter and led her out of the trailer. Rob took the rope so Cha could pick up a jug of water and a plastic bucket. Rob led the way and the donkey followed, no doubt glad to move around. Rob pointed out items of interest about the village as they walked toward the green pasture behind the cottage. After securing the donkey within the fenced area and providing water, Rob brought Cha to the front of the charming cottage. To Cha, it looked like a picture from a storybook.

As she looked through the windows, Cha felt a flutter deep inside her chest. She loved the space and her head whirled with ideas to make it her own. "Yellow," she mused, "definitely yellow with purple trim."

"It could use some paint," he said. "I'll take care of any changes."

"Really? May we go inside?"

"Sure. I own it."

Sensing her delight, he produced a set of keys and unlocked the door. She wondered what other delights awaited. He stepped back for her to enter. His manners impressed.

Cha gave a cry of joy as she saw the well-kept wooden floors imbued with a lovely, aged patina. In the front room, generous windows afforded plenty of natural light. Her eyes followed the staircase against the right wall leading to the upstairs apartment, where a colorful stained glass window graced the exterior wall. Cha closed her eyes and visualized sitting with her morning coffee, the sun sending colorful beams through the stained-glass window. A serving counter divided the kitchen from the main room instead of the usual solid wall, which she noted with approval. The open kitchen would make it easier to serve her customers.

As she walked through each room, she made approving exclamations as she touched the paneled doors, window sashes, and banister. "Oh, look at these ceiling fans!" she said, before realizing, in all likelihood, Rob had installed them. He commented on her appreciation for the small details some missed. Thoroughly delighted, Cha wandered into the kitchen, taking in the built-in shelves, large pantry, and accessible electrical outlets. Above the work island hung a large oval iron caddy meant for hanging pots, though she thought it perfect for drying herbs. The sink in the back of the kitchen faced a blank wall.

"I've always envisioned a window there so you can see the sunsets. I'll put one in, if you'd like."

Cha turned to him with a blinding smile. "I'm home," she said. "I'll take it, and the windows, and the pasture, and the shed for Ariabella, this marvelous kitchen, and the beautiful wood floors. Is it available? I mean, now?"

"You haven't seen the upstairs," Rob laughed. "Let's go up there."

As she climbed the stairs, the smooth, wooden banister slid under her hand. The loft apartment had a steep-pitched roof that formed the walls. Cha walked through, her hands outlining each corner and window frame. Overhead, she imagined the exposed beams lined with hooks full of drying herbs, and decorating possibilities for the dormers came to mind.

"This old fireplace hasn't warmed anyone's feet in years," Rob said. "It can be given a new life with a little stone work."

"Everything's so cozy and inviting. I just love it! I'm sure I'll be right at home here. I'll start right now, if you'll allow me."

Rob looked pleased. "Tonight? There's no bed."

Cha laughed. "I have a sleeping bag. I can buy a bed tomorrow." She knew Rob's startled look probably had something to with the fact that she hadn't asked about the price. It didn't matter. They would agree and the place would soon be hers. *Maybe you were right, Father, the rainbow ends here in Divine.*

"Okay, it's a deal!" Rob held out his hand to shake on their business agreement. Cha put her hand in his, and they stood connected with hands and eyes locked, each rooted to the spot.

Rob spoke first. "This calls for a special toast. Tell you what, while you bring over your wagon, I'll pick up a bottle of champagne and meet you back here in fifteen minutes. Divine is not that big," he added with eyes twinkling.

They walked downstairs and Cha thought, *this is what it feels like to be excited about life!* "I'm going to check on Ariabella first to make sure the shed is comfortable for her."

Rob smiled. "Not a problem. We will make sure her new home meets with your requirements." Rob took her by the elbow to assist her out the side door to the pasture. They watched Ariabella chase a lone firefly in the soft twilight.

Rob stood so close that his breath stirred Cha's hair. "I also chase fireflies." They laughed. "She looks content. Maybe she knows this will be her new home."

They walked across the pasture to the shed. Ariabella trotted over and joined them in inspecting her night quarters, giving an approval with an *awweeah-aweeah!* Cha gave Ariabella a reassuring hug. The donkey went back to chasing fireflies and Rob and Cha parted for the moment.

Cha retrieved her wagon and pulled into the driveway next to the cottage. "Home! I'm home!" The words sounded so good.

She started to bring in her things, but stopped to find a few candles. She lit them; daylight was passing into night. She reached for a notebook and pen. Ideas flooded her mind, and she couldn't write fast enough to keep pace with her racing thoughts. She noticed Rob's name appearing in her notes. "As if I need a reminder!"

Rob walked in carrying champagne, a basket with two glasses, fruit, and cheese. "I took the liberty of settling in your pet with hay and grain from the trailer."

"How sweet!" Cha set down her notebook and spread a quilt on the floor for the impromptu picnic.

Rob said, "Ariabella seems happy and secure. What about you, beautiful? Are you happy?"

"I am so thankful; my heart is about ready to burst."

They enjoyed a candlelight supper on the floor and toasted their alliance.

Cha raised her glass. "To home, to learning, to love and living life."

"Cheers!"

They clinked glasses and sipped the champagne. Cha had unending questions about Divine and the surrounding areas, and Rob was more than happy to tell her. He continued until she stifled a yawn.

"I'm not used to champagne. In fact, it's a first; it's very nice."

Rob took her hand to help her up from the floor.

"Rob, you have made our entrance into Divine exactly that, simply divine! I hate to admit I'm sleepy this early in the evening, but it's been a long day with so many new experiences. I'm overwhelmed… all these new emotions."

"Get a good night's sleep. I'll get your electricity turned on early and come by tomorrow after work to check on you. Then we can talk business."

He removed a key from his keychain. "Your key." She took it with a deep sense of satisfaction. "I'm glad it was you, Cha. Sweet dreams." He closed the door behind him.

She had a floating sensation. *If I dream of you, how could it be oth-*

erwise? Suddenly, everything seemed too perfect: the shop, the living space, the town, the cottage, *that man!* Her thoughts jumbled her past life with her present. Rob seemed up front and open with his feelings, while with her parents it was constant guesswork. The picture they presented to the world was a lie. And now, with everything laid before her, it seemed too easy, perhaps deceptively so. With her limited experiences, she didn't have faith in her judgment. Questions crowded her happiness and doubts crept in, including whether Rob would return the next day.

Cha brought several candles to the little fireplace and placed them inside. She got on her knees and prayed. "Dear God, you didn't choose to bless my childhood. Well, now is your chance to make me a true believer. This rapture inside me is real. Everything in my soul says, 'Rob, you are part of my future.' God! Let me see his sweet, kind face tomorrow. I am ready to accept all blessings you give me, this cottage, and the pasture for Ariabella." She took a moment of silent meditation.

Having said her piece to God, she got up off her knees and prepared to camp out in her new home. "Sweet dreams," she said. She closed her eyes, surrounded by a lifetime of dreams.

CHAPTER THIRTEEN

I Give Myself Permission

Cha awoke to the pink light of dawn, feeling rested and excited all at once. The burden of finding a place had resolved itself upon her arrival in Divine. She could scarcely wait to get started. First, she needed to check on Ariabella, who had both a fun-loving nature and an independent streak. Cha felt certain the donkey's intelligence, mixed with determination, helped her survive an abusive past.

Ariabella did not want to leave the stall, so Cha went about cleaning it anyway, working around the donkey until everything looked good. Cha gave her a kiss on her stubborn nose and said, "I understand, Ariabella, a girl must assert herself every now and then." She applied healing salve to the donkey's sores and left her a hearty breakfast.

Cha returned to the cottage, showered, and braided her lavender-scented hair. She dressed in a long, flowing skirt and a peasant blouse in shades of green, tied a green-paisley-fringed scarf at her waist, put on her majorette boots, and topped off the outfit with a pair of turquoise earrings. Dressed for the occasion, she walked downstairs to begin her first day in Divine.

"There's no time like the present," she said as she entered the kitchen, ready to go to work. She brought in her cleaning supplies and baking equipment from the station wagon. Donning an apron, she gave the kitchen a thorough cleaning before shelving a few ingredients and placing items from her cooler into the refrigerator.

She decided to start her entrepreneurial career with something aromatic, yet simple—lemon poppy seed muffins. She mixed up the batter and loaded a double batch into the sparkling oven. She threw open the doors and windows to air out the rooms and let passers-by know the cottage was coming to life after being closed. She washed her new coffee urn, then put together a makeshift "Open" sign and stuck it in the front window. Soon, the smell of coffee and baking muffins filled the shop and the street outside, advertising what was going on indoors.

Grateful to have studied calligraphy in art class, she printed her limited menu on the inside of a muffin box, making it appear larger than it was. "Not bad," she said as she propped the sign on the counter.

As she worked away, ideas came for all manner of things. She retrieved the string of Tibetan prayer bells, which had hung from the door of her father's garden shed, and tied them to the front doorknob. She checked on the muffins and put them on a rack to cool.

"Hello?"

Cha turned. It was the postmaster who presented her with a large bunch of flowers.

"Thank you!"

"Will you look at this! I am betting those muffins taste as good as they smell. Welcome to Divine, Miss Cha. Rob has been spreading the word of our beautiful new citizen."

"The flowers are lovely. Yes, I'm Cha, and you are…?"

After introductions, the postmaster ordered coffee and a muffin to go. Cha was thrilled. Her first sale! A few locals came by to introduce themselves and sample her muffins. It was all she could do to break away to bake more and keep the coffee urn from running out. Time slipped away. She met many well-wishing neighbors, and felt positive they would be regular customers and friends. Plus, Rob had publicized her and the shop. Yes!

Light-headed with the success of her first efforts, she sold every single muffin, exhausted her ingredients, and almost ran out of napkins. She closed the shop at three o'clock.

Baking while running a shop took more work than her little muffin stand back on the farm. Though not averse to hard work, Cha recognized the need for an extra set of hands. She made another sign advertising for part-time help, and placed it in the front window.

"Mercy!" she declared, "I'm already expanding!"

She planned a menu for the next day and made a shopping list. Finally, sitting down for a rest, she wondered if she had taken on too much. There was still more work to be done. She got up and washed the muffin pans, tidied the kitchen, and then notated her cash intake, the ingredients used, and their cost. Cha went upstairs for her handbag. There would be no muffins of any kind without a trip to the grocery store. Rob's smile came to mind as she recalled how he told her the town wasn't big.

She stepped outside and Ariabella trotted to the fence at Cha's call. "Bye for now," she said. "Wherever the grocery store is, it can't be too far."

Cha saw that Rob had unhitched the trailer and moved it to the side. "Oh, you're a good one, you are." She chuckled as she got in. "Woody hasn't been unloaded and I'm already in business."

Divine had quaint cottages and brick zigzag sidewalks, but didn't have the flavor of an old town. It was alive with citizens who walked and talked fast, unlike the southern town she grew up in where people moved at a pace that seemed to indicate nothing very important was going to happen when they did reach their destination. She found the people in town to be courteous, helpful, and curious. They expressed joy in everyday things.

She dropped a postcard in the mail to Mr. Levy to tell him she had arrived safely and to let him know she had started her new life in the beautiful town of Divine. Next, she went to City Hall to inquire about running her business. The white Georgia marble building sat on top of a hill at the end of Main Street. As she climbed the numerous steps, she thought, *this is symbolic—each step moves me upward.* Inside City Hall, Cha had an informative discussion with the office clerk about her home and business. The clerk said, "Perhaps you have rushed into sales before applying for a business license." Cha filled out the necessary paperwork to make things right and legal.

Next, she went to the feed and seed store, where she had an in-depth conversation with the owner, Mr. Crowley, about Ariabella's diet. The sweet gentleman sported worn, clean and pressed overalls, and a welcoming smile. She selected a number of healthy potted herbs for the cottage's front window boxes. Remembering how customers used to bring their pets to the farm stand, she bought a bag of kibble and a box of dog biscuits. After purchasing several bags of potting soil and two large sacks of crushed barley, Cha and Mr. Crowley laughed together in the parking lot as they had to shift things around in the wagon to get everything in. He offered to drop off the alfalfa hay for Ariabella. Cha placed a standing order for a weekly delivery. Before she left, she used Mr. Crowley's phone to call the telephone company and ordered service.

On her last stop, she bought a generous supply of groceries, fitting them in the remaining space in her wagon. As Cha pulled into the driveway of her cottage, she felt as though she had done it a hundred times before. She sat for a moment and admired the miracle of her journey.

She had no reservations about buying the property; it was meant to be hers. She intended to put a check in Rob's hands as soon as he named his asking price, realizing the deal was between them. She didn't have to ask for anyone's permission.

Cha was putting her purchases away in the kitchen when the Tibetan bells jingled. A thin, dark-haired young woman stepped into the shop. "Hello?"

Cha responded, "Back here! I'm out of muffins, but do come in."

The young woman strode toward the back of the shop, and with hands on hips said, "I'm in good health and I want your part-time job. Sage, my boy, is five years old. He has a medical condition that limits his growth. He's had all the teasing he can take and now he refuses to go to school. He knows stuff, my little Sage."

When the young woman paused for a breath, Cha extended her hand in greeting. "I'm Cha Vickery, and you are…?"

"Etta Riggs. Nice to meet you. The man I've been caring for died a few days ago. The family turned us out and we've been sleeping in an abandoned school bus behind Mr. Crowley's feed store. Miss Cha, we are out of money. Please give me a chance at whatever you need me to do. Please."

Cha could tell Etta's pleading eyes told only part of the story. "Etta, I'll make tea. Have a seat on the stairs and I'll join you shortly."

Cha took a moment to process Etta's situation, as well as her own. Cha needed help in the shop, but wasn't expecting two live-ins. Where would she put them? The young woman seemed desperate. The shop held great promise, but this was a bigger responsibility than she intended. The boy's plight tugged at her heart. How could she turn them away? But again, how could she risk her fledgling business with someone she didn't know? She put away the rest of her groceries and thought hard. As the teakettle whistled, she made her decision. Cha brought over the tea.

"Etta, my living quarters are modest, but I believe we can manage. It's unfurnished, as you can see. I only pulled into town yesterday, but I saw a second-hand furniture store, and we'll just make do with what there is until we work things out. I'll give you the chance you're asking for on a trial basis. There will be rules you'll have to agree to."

"Oh, Miss Cha, thank you! You'll never regret this decision, I promise. We won't let you down."

Cha took some money from her handbag and gave it to Etta. "Here. Take Sage to that little bed and breakfast down the street, and stay there for tonight. Rest up, then we'll work out our agreement tomorrow. There's much to be done."

Etta left, closing the door behind her with the tinkling of the prayer bells. "Prayer wouldn't be such a bad idea," Cha murmured to herself. "What have I gotten myself into?"

Cha tried to organize her thoughts. The bells on the door sounded again, and Rob walked in with a big grin. "You hiring?"

Cha brightened. "You're too late. I just hired somebody. Guess I better remove that sign. Thanks for putting the word out. I sold everything I had." She smiled at him.

"I knew you wouldn't be able to wait," Rob laughed. "Feel like sharing supper with me tonight? I'd like to hear more about you."

"I'm so glad you're here. I committed myself to an employee and two houseguests. I'm wrung out and the wagon still needs to be unloaded. Want to help?"

Rob pitched in and carried larger loads. The job was finished in less time than she imagined. Again, Cha spread her quilt and they picnicked on the floor. They talked about the house and, as Cha imagined, everything went as she hoped.

When they finished their food, Cha took a deep breath. They clinked beer cans and after a few sips, Cha sensed a shift. She focused on Rob and his handsome features. "Hi," she said. She imagined what it might be like to kiss him, but wasn't sure he was feeling the same thing. "Let's go for a walk and check on Ariabella. I'll tell you what's happened around here today." Then she stopped. First, she needed to confirm her feelings were being returned. She reached for his wrist and faced him. "Rob, I am new at being a woman, and I don't want to waste another minute of my life. I have to be upfront—does this attraction between us look as promising to you as it does to me?"

Rob put his arm around her. "Yes, it does." He gave her a squeeze. "Let's walk outside and wait for the fireflies."

Ariabella munched on grass and was not distracted by their presence. Cha was pleased that her pet was getting used to her new home. She would check on her again the next day.

As Rob and Cha walked, talked, and listened, it wasn't long before desire passed between them. Rob was absorbed in her every word, and she felt important and valued in his presence.

As they watched the fireflies, Cha said, "It's all about love and finding the right firefly, one mesmerized by your sparkle. It's an aerial dance to attract a mate." The glittering lights made for a romantic setting beneath the canopy of stars, and they continued to talk until the hour grew late.

Cha felt the harmony between them, so natural and good. There, in the moonlight, Rob took her into his arms and kissed her. She felt the romance, the feel of him, the passion and gentleness of his mouth, his beard on her face. She felt her body grow weak and she trembled.

"It's okay, Cha. You can trust me."

She did. He held her close and the warmth of his body was in contrast to the cool night air. The smell of his skin combined nicely with the freshness of dewy grass. It filled her senses. Field crickets played their love songs and Cha felt romance swirl around her. She wanted to be with him, to experience all of him. She knew the old rules stated that a lady should be a lady—always, but it seemed wrong, like advice for an earlier point in time, or for a different situation. Loving him seemed right and she wanted to make love with him.

Without a word, he led her back to the pasture. Beneath the stars and the moon and leaves of the trees, he coaxed her onto her back on the soft grass. He kissed her passionately and as a mature woman, she responded in kind. He moved his hands over her clothes, exploring her curves. Cha also wanted to feel a man, this man. She knew he would want her to touch his broad shoulders and muscular arms.

His kisses transported her. Over all, she felt safe in his arms and a readiness as her body responded to his touch, but at the same time, her doubts rose to the surface, even as she tried to push them away. Was she rushing things? Should she have sex this very night? Would it hurt? What was she supposed to do? She didn't know. There was never anyone to ask, never anyone to tell her. He pulled away.

"Is something wrong?" he asked. He held her face with his work-roughened hands. "What are these, tears? I only want to bring you happiness."

"I am a thirty-two-year-old virgin."

"Oh, Cha, don't be afraid. I care for you. I know we haven't known each other long, but all I can imagine is spending more time with you. I love being near you, seeing you, hearing your stories. I promise I will not hurt you. Shhh." He hushed softly, kissing her forehead and bringing her closer in an embrace that quelled her fears.

"I want to experience all the wonders that life has to offer. I do trust you."

"Cha, you are a beautiful woman, inside and out. Tell me what you want."

"You."

"Are you sure?"

"Yes." *I give myself permission*, she thought.

"Let's go inside."

He stood and helped her up. He held her hand as they walked into the cottage. They went upstairs and Cha lit her candles. She took a moment to freshen up and joined him by the candlelight. He was handsome and her heart yearned to experience love in all its wonders. She felt she could trust him with her feelings and her body. Spreading out a quilt, they lay down together. He brought her close and any remaining misgivings she had melted away. There was no awkwardness as he removed her clothing as well as his own.

"You're beautiful," he whispered.

His hands slid up her back and his fingers threaded into her hair. Ready as she would ever be, Cha let the night unfold. Rob proved to be a gentle, loving guide as she explored this new territory, and they sealed their heart connection with their shared desire.

Moonbeams cast upon them through a window dormer as they lay together as one. There was no need to talk. All was complete as they spooned in contentment.

CHAPTER FOURTEEN

A Compassionate Gift

Early the next morning, she felt Rob's kisses dot her face. He was dressed and left with a comment about building a bed. Never in her wildest dreams would she have expected this turn in her life.

Cha showered, dressed, and walked to the mirror. She looked the same, except for the beaming smile that looked back at her, and she felt different. She sat on the stairs to savor her unbelievable night. She had not known what to think about love, only that there was a void in her life. Now a door opened to expose that void—a man's arms holding her, wanting her, and she wanting him, fueling her desires and satisfying them, too. She wanted more of the joyfulness they shared and the feelings that still surged through her body. She had allowed herself to know what love could be, its potential as a wonderful part of life, and not as a burden as she had seen with her parents. They were connected by marriage, not by the heart.

"Well, Mother," she said, "you were wrong! It is more than what one sees in the movies!"

She luxuriated in the warmth of his touch that still lingered in her body when a loud knock brought her to attention. Cha called out from the stairs, "I'll be right down!" Scurrying to the front door, she saw it was Etta, holding a suitcase. A young boy wearing a backpack stood at her side. Both looked very sleepy.

"Please, come in. You must be Sage," she said to the child. "You can call me Miss Cha. Etta, there's juice and eggs in the fridge. Help yourself. I have to take care of my donkey, Ariabella. When I come back in, we can get started."

Ariabella greeted her with a nuzzle. Cha scratched the precious donkey between her ears and asked, "Do you think God is testing us? We have paid our dues, and here we are starting over. I've met a wonderful man, and now I'm taking in this broken family. Am I doing the right thing?" Ariabella edged her nose into the crook of Cha's arm and paused, as if giving her a hug. Cha felt love fill her heart. Was that the answer?

Cha fed and watered her pet and went back to her shop, uncertain. The shop was quiet, as if the two weren't there. The boy had fallen asleep in the corner, covered by his thin jacket, his worn cap in one hand. His hair was a mass of blonde ringlets. The question in Cha's heart fell away.

Etta approached her. "Thanks for the night at the B and B. We enjoyed a good dinner and a comfortable room. Sage took a long time getting asleep because he was excited about moving in here. I don't sleep much anyway, but Sage needs his rest."

Cha could feel Etta's anguish, and compassion swelled in her heart. She said, "We have a lot to discuss, but for now, take Sage upstairs and put him on my sleeping bag. If you would like to nap, feel free. There is an extra robe on the bathroom shelf. You can use the washer and dryer, and the shower when you need to."

Cha put her arm around the girl's bony shoulder. "It'll be okay, Etta."

"We won't disappoint you, Miss Cha. Sage will love being here. He will win your heart, and Ariabella's, too."

Etta picked up Sage as if he weighed no more than a sack of beans and carried him upstairs. Her petite frame did not look strong.

Cha thought about the herbs she had purchased yesterday and decided how she might use their healing power for her two new housemates. "Today I will make Over all Healing Green Pistachio Muffins and Dinosaur Dark Chocolate Muffins for Sage."

She brought several into the house, tied a small bunch of herbs on the string of the Tibetan prayer bells and saved a few for the stair banister.

She jumped when the phone rang, not expecting service to have started already. It was Rob.

"How did you get the number so quickly?" she asked.

"It's a small town."

The remark made her smile, but then she expressed her concerns. "Etta, the girl I hired yesterday, showed up with her son right after you left. They have no place to live. I offered to let them stay with me." Cha waited through a long pause. "You there?"

"Yes. Cha, it's your choice. Follow your gut. Your heart and your head can mislead you, but your gut will steer you right. At least mine does. I will stop by later. It was not easy leaving you this morning."

"My feelings, too. Anytime is a good time for a visit from you."

Rob hung up. Cha was glad he would stop by. She realized she missed him. She dashed upstairs to get ready for the day.

Having an untrained employee slowed her down. Cha was late getting her menu posted and customers were starting to enter the shop.

An older man in work overalls came in and said, "Give me two of whatever I'm smelling. And a coffee." The Divine townsfolk seemed busy. They spoke their desires, and went on their way with a warm smile.

Through the front window, Cha noticed a soft, misty rainfall. She baked muffins while Etta took over making coffee and waiting on customers. They fell into a rhythm of doing whatever was needed, and by the end of the morning, Cha had to admit having an extra pair of hands was helpful. Etta was a fast learner.

When Cha caught a break, the yellow stuffed dinosaur on the shelf caught her eye. She had put many of her items from garage sales, her "treasures to share," on the kitchen shelves until she could figure out where everything would best suit her.

"I'll be right back," she said to Etta. "Somebody needs this."

She went up the stairs two at a time. Sage sat on the pallet. When he saw her, he ran over to Cha and hugged her around the legs.

"I love you, Miss Cha. I'll love Ariabella, too. And I love this place. Thank you for giving us a warm place to sleep. I didn't like that old yellow school bus."

Cha's heart melted. She held the dinosaur out to Sage. He looked at it, his smile saying, "For me?" He wrapped his arms around it, and plopped back down on the bed covers. Cha knelt.

"I brought you a strong, protective friend who will stay right by your side. You can name him. Are you hungry? Here, I brought you a Power Muffin. Now get some sleep and take your new buddy with you. Sweet dreams."

Sage sleepily grinned up at her and said, "Dino, the Brave One."

"That's a wonderful name." Cha tucked him in. Sage pulled Dino close. He picked off a piece of muffin for himself and a crumb for Dino.

As she stepped downstairs, Cha remembered she had not put out food or water on the sidewalk for customers' pets. She fixed up a bowl of kibble and filled a large bowl of water, and took them out front. There was always something to do next. Customers kept coming, so she mixed up bowl after bowl of batter for muffins. The Tibetan prayer bells jingled again and again as the front door never stopped moving, and neither did Cha and Etta.

The jingling bells had a pleasing sound and meant business. *Rob must be at it again,* she thought with a grin. She was grateful for the steady stream of customers, and also that she had the foresight to get help. The mood in the shop was spirited. Everyone who entered brought smiles, hugs, and welcoming messages. Cha recognized some as repeat customers. She was thrilled as now they weren't buying only one muffin, but a dozen.

By three o'clock, sales began to taper off. At three-thirty, it was quiet. Cha put up the "Closed" sign. She recognized an evolving pattern that would help establish her shop's hours of operation. She made the decision to close the shop to customers at three o'clock.

More work would follow. Cha and Etta set about cleaning the kitchen. As Etta swept up, Cha made notations in her journal. There were numerous entries for income and outgo. When she counted the day's take from the cash drawer, she thought, *Father, you would be so proud of me, and Mother, I believe you would, too!*

Etta completed her work. "What else would you like me to do, Miss Cha?"

"I believe we're through for today, Etta. Good work! Why don't you go upstairs and rest? We will do this all over again tomorrow, bright and early."

Etta thanked Cha again for the opportunity to work and headed upstairs.

Later, Sage appeared on the stairs, hugging his new yellow dinosaur friend close to his small body. "Miss Cha, Dino was having bad dreams. I protected him. Mean kids were teasing and threw rocks at him, but I gave him a bite of my Power Muffin and he grew big muscles and the two of us chased them away." His voice was thick with sleep.

"I see. Come into the kitchen, Sage, you need a regular meal. What do you like to eat?"

"Mashed potatoes."

"Well, how about some meatloaf, vegetables, and lots of mashed potatoes," Cha said with a big smile.

"Okay!"

"My friend Rob will be here later, and when he comes, you can help us feed and brush Ariabella. She'll need fresh straw before her bedtime." Cha reached out and felt Sage's arm muscle. "Are you strong enough?"

Sage grinned. Cha gave him a glass of milk to drink as she set about preparing his food.

Cha wanted her shop to be a place where people would linger, relaxing with friends over muffins and coffee. She planned to put up a neighborhood bulletin board with a sign welcoming people to write comments. She had seen this in a small farm town, and thought it a wonderful idea. The front sidewalk would have small white lights surrounding it, and with new paint, she was sure the storefront would be an attractive gathering place.

She needed to run errands and wondered whether or not she could leave the shop with Etta for a couple of hours. Etta had worked hard. All looked promising for the shop and her life.

Sage brought Cha his empty glass. "Miss Cha, I can help a whole lot. I saw Ariabella out the window. I told her I would be her best friend."

"Ariabella likes having friends who love her. A bad man worked her hard and then called her lazy. He was mean to her. Those days are over. She is happy now."

"I will make her happy. She is a sweet donkey and I will call her sweet names. Miss Cha, I told her I slept in an ugly old school bus and she said I could sleep with her."

"Oh? Sage. I'm sure you will be a good friend. Ariabella's wounds are healing nicely."

The good meal brought Sage to life and he chattered as he ate. "Ariabella said that God sent her to you because you were lonely and needed a best friend. What do you think, Miss Cha, can I stay? I need you to be my friend, too."

Cha thought, *can this little one also have a special gift for understanding animals?* Cha smiled down into the young boy's large amber eyes, his delicate, wise face surrounded by golden blond curls. Sage looked back up at her with his earnest, pure expression.

"Sage," she said, "we are all on a journey. I am glad your journey brought you here, and I'm sure Ariabella will be your friend."

"Thank you, Miss Cha."

Cha understood the need for love and approval. "When I was a little bit older than you, I worked with my father in his gardens. Only it wasn't so much like work—I loved being there. The herb garden was my favorite. One day, my father overheard me talking to a marsh rabbit. The rabbit was scared and angry because I had almost stepped on her babies. She accepted my apology and showed them to me. To make up for it, I broke off a stack of lettuce for her.

"While we were talking, my father came to my side. He took my hands in his and said, 'You have been given a special gift, as I have. Your heart opened up so that you can hear the animals. We must honor this gift. We have been called upon to protect all living things.' And then he said, 'We share this secret. Others do not understand.' When he told me that, I knew it was true."

Cha held Sage's hands as her father had held hers. "Sage, do you understand why I shared my story with you?"

"I do," Sage responded with wisdom tinged with sadness. "I like animals. The kids at school aren't nice to me."

"We can't always understand the people around us. Sometimes people hurt what they don't understand. That's just the way it is." Cha ached for his innocent soul.

At that moment, Etta came downstairs. She had showered and changed into a white tee shirt and cut-off jeans that accentuated her thin, pale body.

Etta took Sage's fork from his hand and ate a bite of his food. "Boy! That's good!" she said as she devoured the rest of what was on his plate.

"Miss Cha made this food for me. I was saving it for later," Sage protested. "Miss Cha loves me and wants me to stay. But my Etta also needs a good meal so we will both be strong."

"Thanks, my little Sage," Etta responded. She patted him on the head.

Cha could tell Sage felt bad he annoyed his mother. She watched the two closely. Sage was skin and bones, like his mother. His demeanor changed when Etta came into the room. He was guarded now, defensive and closed, when a moment ago he had been open and trusting.

Sage picked up Dino and held on tight. His face looked as though a dark cloud had moved across the sun.

"Etta, why don't you take Sage to the pasture to spend some time with Ariabella? Keep your distance these first few days so she can get to know you. I need to run a couple of errands, and when I get back, we can have some tea and a nice, long chat."

Sage perked up. "Can I take Dino out to meet her?"

"Of course," Cha said. "She'd love to meet Dino. Have fun!"

Cha watched as Etta took Sage outside. Cha wanted to give her the benefit of the doubt. Her uncertainty remained and would have to be explored later. She considered Rob's words, "Trust your gut." That wouldn't be easy. She went upstairs to her father's old attaché case and took out most of the remaining cash. She grabbed her handbag and headed out.

Her first stop was the antique store. She had acquired her mother's good taste and passion for antiques and purchased a few tables and chairs to be delivered for the shop, as well as pieces for her own use. Each piece held its own character and she imagined how charming the mismatched chairs would look when arranged as a group. She opened an account at the bank and deposited the remaining funds.

When Cha returned, she saw Etta had made sandwiches. Sage sat on the counter as the two women ate standing up.

Sage asked, "Miss Cha, do you think Ariabella will give me a ride someday?"

Cha replied, "It's possible. She still has raw spots and doesn't like anyone touching her unless I'm there. She likes her pom-poms. They're nice and light, like you. For now, she should feel free. Sage, would you like to visit her again?"

Sage hopped off the counter. "Oh, yes, may I?" She noted Sage deferred to her and not his mother.

"Stand outside the fence and let her come to you." Cha said.

He dashed outside, clutching Dino.

"Can we talk now?" Etta said. "We've only just met so I understand your distrust of having two strangers living in your house."

Cha felt eager to get started. Sage's presence brought an indescribable sweetness and filled a place she had not known was lacking, but Etta's tone made her wonder if her distrust shouldn't take precedence.

CHAPTER FIFTEEN

Etta's Agreement

Cha made tea and brought it to the staircase where they sat. Etta's face, even with her tired eyes and flat expression, was hard to read.

Taking a deep breath, Etta said, "My mother told me I was born bad. I dreamed of a different life without her. Mother existed off the good will of anyone who gave her drugs or whiskey. I never knew my father. I left home at twelve; it was my only chance for survival. I never saw or spoke to her again.

"She taught me her cunning ways, and it came in handy. I took up with street people I met at the Greyhound bus station. They knew the safe places to sleep and get food. These people were my family, but I moved around a lot. When I turned sixteen I got a job working in a cheap bar. After work, we'd all sit around and drink. There were times I blacked out from drugs and whiskey. Some of the things I do remember, I'm ashamed of.

"Thankfully, the police found me one night. I was half out of it, almost frozen, curled in a ball on the street. It was sleeting. Someone covered me with a black plastic garbage bag. I was sick—delirious!"

Etta sighed. "Those cops saved my life. They placed me in a detox center for indigents. I stabilized, but then I discovered I was pregnant. Knowing that helped me stop cold turkey. The doctors pressured me to have an abortion. It was horrible. They said I'd caused serious damage already and that I'd probably lose the baby. I had lost control of my life, but the one thing I could control was to say no to the abortion. I fought like a lion to keep that baby, even though they said social services would take the baby anyway.

"One of the attending nurses took pity on me. She offered me a place to live and said she would take care of my living expenses in exchange for adopting my baby. She said she could handle it if the baby had problems, like from the drugs I took. She assured me he would get the best care, so after my detox, I moved in with her. She lived up to her agreement. It seemed to be the best solution."

Cha nodded and hummed in acknowledgment, but didn't interrupt. She didn't want to place judgment on Etta's actions, not knowing or guessing how anyone would or should behave in the same situation.

Etta continued. "Sage was premature and weighed only three pounds. I used to look at him through the incubator, and my heart was overcome with shame because I jeopardized his health. This tiny little baby—my baby—struggling to live. I loved him so much! I was still only sixteen with no job, no prospects, and no family, just Sage. My nurse friend and I, we supported each other, not knowing whether Sage was going to make it. Somehow, he pulled through. For whatever reason, God had given me this angel. I started to resent my friend for thinking Sage was hers."

"But you gave your word."

"At that moment, my word meant nothing. I would have said anything." Etta's eyes held a fierce determination and Cha did not doubt her for a second.

"I believe you tried to do the right thing by the old gentleman you took care of here in Divine. Did that experience change you?"

"Let me tell you the rest. When the nurse started calling him, Thomas, after her father, instead of Sage, I knew there was problem.

The day we brought Sage home, my friend walked in with papers for me to sign to make it official. I told her I wanted one night and that I'd sign in the morning. It was a lie. There was no way I could leave Sage!

"When she was asleep, I wrapped up Sage in his crib blanket. I took her money and left in the black night, not one star in the sky. Didn't even leave a note! I took my tiny baby, knowing he had special needs and not knowing how I was going to care for him. We got a bus and left the state. I felt for sure she would have me arrested for taking her money, but I never heard from her or the police."

Cha's thoughts raced to places she wished they wouldn't go. Etta used someone who helped out in her time of need. She didn't express regret for stealing or going back on her word. Cha hoped something had happened in the past five years that would have turned Etta's life around so these questions and doubts would go away, and yet, she was overcome by something more, that there was a reason Etta and her cherished, innocent boy walked into her shop.

"I got money from panhandling. I'll admit holding a baby helped bring in the dollars. I rented cheap rooms and stayed in women's shelters; they were kind to us. Whenever Sage got sick, I found a hospital where they couldn't turn us away. We managed.

"It never bothered me to have others step in and provide for my little Sage. Anyone who set their eyes on him would love him and want to help. He's so beautiful, my Sage, inside and out. Often, I wonder, why me? God, you entrusted this wonderful child into my care. What did God see in me? I must not be so bad after all."

"Etta, do you feel responsibility for the choices you have made?"

"What difference does it make?" Etta contorted her face into a puzzled look, causing deep wrinkles in her young face.

Cha nodded. She had a home and food to eat. She was never in a position where she had to scramble to stay alive. Etta did what she could to provide shelter and meals for herself and a child in tow, which was not so hard to understand. Etta had used him, but it was for their mutual benefit. Something brought them to her doorstep, making her believe it was the right decision to take them in. Lost in her thoughts, Cha refocused as Etta continued.

"In his way, my little Sage helped me as much as I helped him. He knows things before they happen. He has an odd gift; he communicates with animals. That's why he likes your donkey. He says animals tell him secrets. One time, outside a motel, Sage saw a stray white cat. He kept after me to feed it, but I didn't. It kept coming back anyway, scratching at the door. Sage begged me, 'My Etta, please let the cat in. She wants to tell us something.' Sage is hard to resist, and when he has something on his mind, he is persistent, so I let that dirty, white cat in and Sage lay on the floor next to it. Sage said, 'We have to leave. There's a fire in the motel.' I went outside and I didn't see anything. I asked Sage how he knew the cat was talking to him, and he said he just knew, and that we had to go. So, I gathered up our stuff, and we went out. Well, then I did smell smoke and pulled the fire alarm! He took the cat. I saw him whispering in its ear as we left. He gave it to a homeless woman who said she'd take care of it. I gave her a dollar and we left for the bus station. I asked the ticket lady at Greyhound how far we could go on my money, and she said Divine, Georgia. I could see the fire from the bus, raging! Sage could see it, too. He thanked me, and then he curled up and went to sleep."

Cha said, "Etta, I believe somehow, some way, our experiences take us where we need to go."

Again, Etta had a quizzical look. Cha believed Etta was telling the truth, even though she admitted to being a liar when it suited her needs. It made Cha wonder…what did Etta believe about her life's path? Cha felt uncomfortable, but let Etta finish.

"Anyway," Etta continued, "someone left a newspaper on the bus, and I saw an ad for a caregiver. We slept overnight in the Divine bus station and in the morning, I called. You probably think I am the most unlikely person to care for another person's welfare, but I am capable of doing most any task when I need to.

"I talked to the man, Mr. Whaley. He was in a wheelchair and said his family was taking advantage. He was very interested when I said I had a young son. Mr. Whaley was such a sweet man, and he enjoyed having little Sage around. After he found out Sage was a good reader, he had Sage read to him. We were there for almost a year. We got along fine, though his family didn't like me much, and when he died they tossed us onto the street without so much as an extra day's pay.

"Mr. Crowley let us sleep in the old school bus behind his store. He paid for our meals at the diner. Sage and I were in there that day you pulled in, and we overheard you talking. When Sage saw you had a donkey in the trailer, he got real excited. He said you would help us, but I thought it was nonsense because you were new in town. The diner folks were talking about your new muffin shop. When I walked in, Sage went around to the side of the building to see your donkey."

Before Cha could say anything, Etta said, "Miss Cha, have you made a decision about us?"

Cha noted Etta's use of the word "us." Etta was skilled at using Sage to manipulate others. "I'll need to think on everything you've said, Etta, and honestly, a few things disturb me, the first being Sage. I am sure you love him and want him to have a safe home, but some of your choices make me think he hasn't been cared for as well as he should be. I am going to take a chance. You and Sage can stay with me and we'll see how things progress. I see you tried to have a stable life with your last live-in situation. My living quarters are small. I'll ask Rob—the man I'm buying the property from—if he can figure out a way to give us more space and privacy.

"In the meantime, Sage can use my sleeping bag and you can

sleep on the sofa that's being delivered tonight. We will share household chores and you can be my shop assistant." Cha's heart was telling her to go ahead, but her gut was screaming caution. "Etta, you've made some frightful choices, but this choice led you to me. I want my business to prosper and I want good things for all of us. I see how your life has been filled with hardship, but you've made it this far. You have Sage and you were right, he has touched my heart.

"I will have house rules. You two are under my roof, and that makes me responsible for you. Sage is not my son, but I am going to offer some guidance, starting with this: I don't like hearing Sage being called "little Sage." He knows he is smaller than the other children his age, and he has to live with their awful teasing. We don't have to add to it. He's coming in. Do you mind if I ask him how he feels about being called *little* Sage?"

Etta shook her head and Cha asked him.

"I don't like it. I'm fine about the way I am." Etta picked him up. Sage said, "My Etta, I am too big to be carried. Put me down!"

Cha observed, "We have our answer. Second, we will be busy working and Sage needs to be in public school. If you like, I can go with you to help him enroll. If we bring muffins for his classmates, he'll get off to a good start. We will deal with any bullying, I promise." Cha understood the pain of feeling left out and would do her best to help Sage fit in.

Etta nodded. "I'm sure it's for the best."

"Let's see how the first month goes. I'm going to give you some cash. Take Sage into town and buy him some school clothes. Buy yourself long skirts or pants for working in the shop. No shorts. Blue jeans are fine."

"Okay, thanks." Etta said she would abide by Cha's conditions and as the two shook hands, Cha noticed Etta's hand quivered.

Cha reached into her handbag and gave Etta money. "This should be enough. Here are the car keys."

"You trust me with your car?"

"Any particular reason I shouldn't? You do drive, don't do?"

"Yes. I can drive, and I'll take good care of your car."

"It was my father's, so it's more than just a car," Cha said.

Etta and Sage left, and the delivery truck stopped in front of the cottage. In minutes, they unloaded the tables, chairs, and other items Cha bought. Cha went into the kitchen to set up for the morning. She looked over her newly stocked ingredients. She made mental notes about what to make the next day, but her mind wandered to her situation. Etta's story was gritty and likely the truth, but how could she know? She guessed most people wouldn't admit to having a drug problem or living on the streets. Etta would still be working for Mr. Whaley if he hadn't died. Choosing to be a caregiver was a thoughtful, responsible choice for her and her son, and it seemed Etta was on the road to turning her life around. Also, she didn't waste any time coming in to the shop and asking—no demanding to be hired. These were all positive signs.

She knew better than anyone that death could bring change, but rather than focus on the negative, Cha decided to shift her thoughts to something bright, like the yellow jonquils she loved so much. The bulbs she sowed where she buried her mother and father would burst into bloom every spring. She hoped they could look upon their beauty. It was unlikely anyone ever escaped the bad memories and pain from their past. We all had to carry on.

Cha heard Rob pull up in his pickup truck. She leaned against the doorframe and felt happy seeing him again as he bounded up the steps. He kissed her and she relaxed.

"You look nice," he said. "I like your necklace, and that braid encircling your head like a crown. Very queenly! How about we have a cold one and you can tell me about your day?"

They went inside and he put his arms around her. His strength made her feel protected, safe, and sexy. Definitely sexy. They kissed and Cha wished it would never stop.

"I've thought about you all day," Rob said.

Cha liked his husky voice. Hearing it made her want to lie with him again. She kissed him and sensed his desire. Yes, the feelings were new, but she understood what she felt.

"I'd take you upstairs if I thought we were alone," he said.

"Etta and Sage have gone shopping," Cha said.

Their eyes widened and they sprinted for the stairs. She laughed all the way up and he swung her around so her feet lifted off the floor. She shrieked with joy, but then his mouth was on hers and the excitement of spontaneity turned to pure desire. Cha reveled in knowing he desired her, listened to her, and missed being with her. She felt gratitude for the moment, for him. She breathed in the manly smell of his skin, musky from work, and called out his name in passion as if she had said it forever.

"Rob," she said as she reached for her clothes, "I decided to let Etta and Sage move in with me. Etta will work and they will live here on a trial basis for one month. I'd like to hear your suggestions as to how we can make private areas for sleeping."

"I suppose I should tell you, there are rumors around town that Etta had some problems. The word is she was arrested for stealing, but I don't know that anything came of it. You could talk with the sheriff. He knows everything and everyone in Divine." He held her face in his hands. "Ordinarily, gossip is not my thing, but it's you we're talking about, and I'm wishing for an 'us.' As far as I know, she took care of old man Whaley for a year without any problems. It wouldn't hurt to ask, just to be sure."

"It's not her fault her caretaker position ended and it seems like she's trying to continue caring for herself and her son. Sage, he's so precious. I feel it's the right thing to do."

"All right then, let's see how we can make this space fit three." He surveyed the area. "On this wall, I can imagine an enclosed bed with storage underneath and a play area for little Sage. This…"

Cha stopped him mid-sentence. "We've decided not to call Sage 'little.' He's very sensitive about it."

"Oh. How about this? I'll make a sign to go over his bed that says, 'Sage's Place.' That sounds more grown up. And he can help me build his bed."

"Really? That's wonderful!"

"I have extra lumber at my place. We can pick it up, and while we're there, I'd like you to meet my mother, Zarah. I told her about you. She asked me, 'When am I going to meet this mysterious woman?' Cha, I have to tell you, the whole town is talking about you. What do you think?"

"Sounds great!"

Downstairs, Rob looked around the dining area. "I like the way you set up the shop. These tables and chairs look familiar."

Cha laughed. "The man at the antique store said some of these came from the sandwich shop. I thought they were perfect! Nice, they were waiting for me. It all came home." The room looked even more charming than Cha expected.

"Let's go," she said. "I'll leave a note for Etta and Sage. We can feed Ariabella on the way out.

CHAPTER SIXTEEN

A Significant Meeting

On the drive, Cha noticed they were headed for the river. "Is your cabin on the river? I want to know everything about you, where you live, your life."

As Rob turned on the radio, he said, "I like country music. How about you? I haven't heard any music in your shop."

"Growing up, Mother never allowed music in our home. Once in a while, my father would hum and she would yell at him to stop, but I liked it. For me, it was a sign he was happy. Once, on Christmas morning, Father defied Mother and gave me a red battery-operated radio. Heavens! I was thrilled when I heard the Grand Ole Opry! Those performers were having fun, and so was the audience. It was magical. I used to play it in the barn loft where Mother wouldn't hear it. That radio was a window into the outside world. I used to polish it and, I know this sounds silly, but I talked to it like a friend. When I was in bed for the night, I'd dream up little stories." She laughed.

"What kind of stories?"

"Well," she said, "there was one story where a shooting star arced across the sky and fell through the upper loft door, right onto my radio. Sparks and rays of light flashed out of the speaker and my radio came to life! Music played and cast a spell on my make-believe animals. In my story, there were all kinds of animals in the barn, but really, we didn't have any. The animals danced and sang along. It made me happy and helped me through some rough patches. I liked living in my pretend world. That country song brought it all back. I want music and childlike play in my life. And real animals, like Ariabella."

"You can do as you please. Play your music, shout out loud, get a whole menagerie if you want. Promise me you'll do it if it will bring you happiness."

Cha laughed, "I will, you have my word."

Rob turned the truck onto a gravel drive. A cabin surrounded by large oak trees came into view. Cha scanned the area. "What a beautiful place! The river is so close, and kind of wild. Is it always like that?"

"Water's up due to all the recent rains."

Two shiny-coated black dogs, Labrador Retrievers, raced toward them, wild with excitement. Rob called to them, fending off their leaping, tail-wagging welcome. "Settle down, girls. There, that's better. Cha, hold your hands out to them so they can smell you. Don't be afraid; they're friendly." Cha did as he instructed. "May I introduce you to my good friends, Ruby and Lady?"

Cha spoke to the dogs softly and petted them while they kissed her hands and pranced around her. Rob made sure the dogs didn't jump on Cha.

"You're in!" Rob said. "They are usually not so quick to accept anyone new. The girls are very protective of me, Zarah, and the property." He added, almost shyly, "And now they will love and protect you."

"I like being around animals. God, it feels good to let them in!"

Cha gave the dogs a final pat and they trotted ahead, leading them to the cabin. Arm-in-arm they strolled the porch so Cha could see the blooming plants and pots overflowing with mosses, ferns, and other greenery. Containers filled every nook and cranny. She was fascinated with the spread of meaningful objects: baskets of beautiful rocks, vases with bird feathers artfully arranged, and hand-thrown ceramic bowls holding an assortment of acorns, nuts, and seedpods sat on a weathered antique library table.

In another corner of the porch was an old, round wooden table adorned with bird nests, bones of various sizes, a pair of deer antlers, water-smoothed broken glass resting in a mussel shell, and bits of driftwood. Cha moved with care, unaware she was "oohing" and "aahing."

After watching her reaction to the treasures, Rob said, "You can be sure each piece has a story."

Cha reached for his hand. "I want to hear every one."

The screen door sang as it opened. A tall, slim woman appeared. Her silvery hair was tied back. She had a dazzling, chiseled, lived-in-face, and its lines enhanced her beauty. She smiled and opened her long arms in greeting. "You must be Cha. I am Zarah." Her voice was rich and smooth as molasses.

As Cha stepped into Zarah's hug, she caught the scent of fresh-cut evergreens. She thought, *I can't remember ever being hugged by a woman.* She felt accepted into their home. Her eyes misted up as her emotions ran strong, and she prayed this would be the beginning of a long, deep friendship.

"It's such a pleasure to meet you," said Cha with a smile. "I was admiring your collection of treasures."

"Choose something, whatever attracts you," offered Zarah. Cha looked around, and then walked straight to a baseball-sized rose quartz specimen. "Ah, very telling," said Zarah as Cha admired the stone. "Excellent! And now, Miss Cha, you have picked the very best gem, my son."

Zarah reached into a faded red metal icebox on the porch and pulled out three beers. "Do come in. Sorry for my appearance. I felt strong enough today to cut some firewood. I enjoy it and it's good exercise. Rob didn't tell me he was bringing you tonight, but delightfully, here you are. Now, give me another hug." Once again, Zarah held out open arms for Cha.

Zarah smiled. She exuded inner strength and Cha could feel her strong arms as Zarah shepherded her into the cabin. Rob beamed as the three of them talked and laughed over drinks.

A handsome, gold and white, longhaired cat lay curled up on a cushion beside the fireplace, basking in the warmth. Rob greeted him. "Motoo." The cat rose and stretched, then sauntered over to rub against Rob's legs.

Zarah said, "Motoo lets us live here with him. He will befriend you in time."

Motoo stepped over to Zarah, who picked him up and crooned in his ear, before covering his furry face with kisses. Zarah put him down and he returned to his cushion, where he began to groom his silky fur, ignoring them.

"Can you two stay for dinner? I made a big pot of chili and a pan of jalepeño cornbread. I just took it out of the oven, all crusty and brown."

Rob looked regretful. "Sorry, Mother. It smells great, but we can't stay. Let's get together next week. Would you take us on a night ride in your canoe? No one does it better, and it would introduce Cha to the river. The full moon is always a good time. I'll bring a picnic supper and we can eat out on the river."

"Before it gets dark, we have to pick up some lumber. I promised to build a bed for a special boy, Sage. Cha opened her home to him and his mother."

Cha noticed the uneasiness in his voice and it looked like Zarah picked up on it, too.

Zarah nodded. "Sounds more interesting with each word. You'll tell me all about it next week. Okay, be off! I'm going to curl up in front of the fire, have some dinner, and finish my sketches. They're for a new line of jewelry with a nature theme. I'll show you my designs when you come next."

"I will look forward to seeing them. A piece of jewelry sets up my day," Cha grinned.

Rob, Motoo, Ruby, and Lady guided Cha to the barn, where the salvaged lumber was stored along with other interesting architectural treasures. After seeing their home, she understood he wasn't an ordinary builder.

"Cha, my houses are built with love and a respect for old wood. Some people think these old bits and pieces are trash, but I see value and charm, and I repurpose them. I hope in time you will love my buildings as I do." Together they pulled the pieces Rob wanted and in no time, were loaded up and ready to go.

"This is so exciting, building a future, building my life! I know you are a major part of my future. And these wonderful animals, too. Look." Motoo purred and rubbed against her legs. "From this point forward, I will always live with animals. Ariabella opened my heart, and now I can't be stopped."

Rob spoke as he picked up Motoo and placed him in Cha's arms. "Why should you deny yourself?" He kissed Cha on the nose. "I love seeing you open up to life." Motoo purred between them.

They made their way back toward Cha's cottage as the last bit of sunlight disappeared.

"Rob, your mother made me feel welcome and accepted. But why would I be surprised? I felt the same when I arrived in Divine and you welcomed me with a full heart. I feel like I have come home. Home. It's a precious word, and I don't use it lightly."

"Ditto," Rob agreed. "My mother is a knowing woman with an alert mind. You get what you see with her. She lives a life of purpose and it's delightful to be around her." He put his hand over Cha's. "Anything else on your mind?"

"Yes. I really want to give Etta and Sage the opportunity for a fresh start. Do you think I acted too soon?"

"You followed your heart and you have a good heart. I don't know about Etta, but that boy needs you, and right now, he is about to be wowed."

Cha held the rose quartz gift in her hand and let the breeze from the open window soothe her nerves. She tried to hold back her fears and squeezed Rob's hand.

"Cha, I am beside you. We will share any troubles ahead. We are a team now."

CHAPTER SEVENTEEN

Change in Plans

T he truck rolled over the fresh gravel leading to the side door of the cottage. Cha noticed the lights were on upstairs and in the shop. "Where is the station wagon?" she said. "If they're still shopping, who's inside?"

Cha shivered and Rob put his hand around her shoulder. Ariabella announced her displeasure with a raspy *aweeah-aweeah!*

"Ariabella sounds upset." Cha let herself out of the truck. "I'll go to her. Aria!" The donkey trotted up. Cha put her in the shed, saw she had food, and opened the shutters so the donkey could see into the shop. Ariabella seemed less agitated with Cha near. Cha stroked her neck and told her she would come back to brush her.

Rob had waited for her. "I'll go in first," he said.

"I want to go in with you. We're a team now, remember?" The main floor was empty, and they walked up the stairs.

Sage's voice came from a hidden location. "Miss Cha?"

"Yes, Sage. Rob and I are here." Sage crawled out of the sleeping bag and ran to Cha. Rob stepped forward and picked him up.

"Sage, are you alone?" said Rob.

"No! Dino is with me. We turned all the lights on, but when I heard something, I hid. Sorry, Miss Cha. Sometimes I'm afraid of the dark."

Cha took Sage while Rob looked around the cottage once more. "Nothing seems out of the ordinary, except Sage is here by himself."

"Sage, where is your mother?" Cha asked.

"She said she had to do more shopping."

Cha rolled her eyes. "Did she feed you first?"

Sage shook his head. "I'm hungry."

"We are, too. Let's all go in the kitchen. Rob, please make him a sandwich and pour a glass of milk. I need to finish tending to Ariabella. I'll be right back."

"I'll take care of Ariabella," Rob offered.

Cha touched his arm. "Thank you. She needs brushing. It will calm her down."

Cha fluffed Sage's hair and they walked downstairs to the shop, where Cha pulled out the sandwich bread. Rob stepped outside and Ariabella brayed.

Sage burst into tears. "My Cha, I didn't take care of Ariabella, and now she won't be my friend anymore."

"It's okay, Sage, she's fine—a little upset, that's all. You can still visit with her and she'll be happy to see you. Please, eat."

After a while, Cha walked to the landing and looked out over the pasture. "God, I am not entitled to this man and the contentment he has brought into my life. There are times when I am also afraid, but you have given me Rob." She placed her hand over her heart and breathed deeply.

Dusting his hands off on his jeans, Rob said, "Ariabella is all settled in." It was the assurance Cha needed. "What's the story here?"

Cha shrugged her shoulders and shook her head, hoping Etta would come back soon. Cha understood it wasn't always easy to shop with a young child, but she would have to reprimand Etta for leaving her child alone in the cottage. She made a mental note for a house rule: Sage must be attended to at all times.

"Sage, did Etta tell you which shop she was going to?"

"No, Miss Cha, she drove away and said I couldn't go." Sage started to cry, but through his tears he said, "I don't think my Etta is coming back. She said you were going to keep me safe. Are you mad?"

He wiped his eyes with the back of his hand. Sage's pleading look reminded her of Ariabella's eyes the day they first crossed paths behind Billy's garage. The most important thing was that Sage felt cared for and safe. Once more, Cha knew her life would change forever.

"No, Sage, I'm not mad. Let's get you into a bath. You can curl up in your sleeping bag with Dino and have a good night's sleep. Tomorrow Rob needs you to be strong. He's going to build a bed for you and he wants you to help."

"For me?" His eyes lit up. "Miss Cha, can we paint my bed blue and red, like Superman?"

"Yes, of course we can," Cha smiled.

Sage stood so tiny, but brave as he faced Rob and said, "Mr. Rob, I'll eat a good breakfast so I'll be mighty and I will work hard. Thank you. I love you, Miss Cha. Ariabella and I will pray for my Etta. Ariabella is happy I'm going to be with her all the time. She tells me things, Miss Cha. You believe me, don't you?"

"Yes, Sage, I believe you," Cha said. "I am sure Ariabella knows you are a true friend."

Rob asked, "Is there anything in the shop that needs to be done?"

"No, I'm ready for the morning, though heaven knows when Etta will come back. I'll think about it tomorrow. Sage, get ready for your bath."

"My Etta told me to give this to you." He handed her a piece of folded paper from his back pocket and went upstairs.

Rob pulled his chair closer to Cha as she read the letter out loud.

Miss Cha,
Sorry about taking your car. I'll leave it somewhere and send you a note so you can pick it up, but my intentions, like my sorry

life, can get lost. I have no plans, just to get as far away as possible and disappear. Sage deserves better than me. He loves you. My prayer is he will have a happy home with you and Ariabella. In the short time you have known Sage, you have discovered how different and special he is. He's very smart and knows stuff before it happens, and even what Ariabella is thinking, if a donkey thinks.

I am sorry about the letdown. I did wish to do right by you. I signed papers making you Sage's guardian. You will find them and his birth certificate in the register. I never knew Sage's father so no one will come looking to claim him. I believe God sent you to care for my dear boy. My hope is you will not report me to the sheriff.

Enclosed is a letter for Sage. He is a good reader, but matters of the heart upset him and you may have to read it to him.

I could not tell Sage I was leaving for good, to look into his eyes—even I can't do that. I have let him down so many times. Someday I hope he understands. Maybe he already knows. The best thing I can give Sage is a chance at the life he deserves. He will have you and Rob, and he needs a good man to show him how to be one. Sage is so in love with Ariabella he would lay his life down to protect her.

Etta

Cha separated a second page, the letter to Sage, and set both on the table with a sigh. "Etta told me about her hard life. She was unhappy and unloved until Sage was born. She seemed sincere about wanting to work and doing the right thing. I felt it was worth taking a risk for Sage's sake."

Rob said, "As crazy as it sounds, maybe she has done the right thing."

"Maybe I should go to him now and let him read his letter. He seems to have a sense she isn't coming back. I'll check on him." Cha rose and went to the stairs. Sage sat on the top step and looked down at her.

Through quivering lips, Sage said, "My Cha, I heard you read my Etta's letter. Would you read my mother's letter to me?"

"Oh, Sage, I am so sorry. Are you okay? I can read it later if you like."

"Please read it now. I'm ready." He sounded mature beyond his years. He stopped trembling as he prepared himself. Cha joined him and gave him a hug.

"Sage, you have a home here. Our home."

"I know," said Sage.

Cha opened the folded paper.

My dear child, Sage,

You will always be my beautiful boy with a beautiful soul. You aren't so little anymore so I hope one day soon you will understand and know that I am doing this because of my great love for you. I hope you feel that. I am giving up, but I am not giving up on you. I found a way for you to be safe and to have a normal life.

God gave me the chance to do the right thing when we sat in that diner and saw Miss Cha with her pretty station wagon pulling Ariabella's trailer. You were fascinated when you saw Miss Cha. Remember? You said, "Look at her red hair, my Etta, she is going to be our friend." You are always so curious about things, and when you saw the wonder of wonders, the beautiful Ariabella, led out of the trailer, you about ran in circles with joy, asking to see the donkey. Somehow, I knew you would find a way to talk to it. I also had a feeling this was the woman who would want to look after you, so I tracked her down. Maybe because we lived on the streets our whole lives, we became more open about reading people.

Miss Cha will take care of everything and answer all your

questions. I know you will be happy and safe, and she will love
you. No more scary rats in the darkness of night.

 See you in heaven. Your mom,

 Etta

 Sage listened to each word of his mother's letter. He said, "Miss
Cha, my Etta won't be coming back. My heart is sad and it feels all
blown up. But Miss Cha," his lips trembled, "I can see my Etta's face
and hear her funny laugh anytime I want to. When I close my eyes
and imagine, I see all things clearly."

 Rob joined them near the top of the stairs. "You are a brave boy,"
Rob said. "Many things in life are beyond our control. I believe your
mother's great love for you makes her want you to be protected in
a way she couldn't. It's why she left you with Cha. Does that make
sense?"

 Sage answered, "Yes." He struggled to keep his eyes open.

 "I think you need your rest," Cha said.

 Sage went to his sleeping bag and in moments he was asleep.

CHAPTER EIGHTEEN

A Knight to Remember

Cha experienced a high point when she opened her shop after arriving in Divine. She thought she was off to a great start. The people were friendly and coming by for muffins. Her relationship with Rob was developing quickly into love, giving her a fulfillment of purpose she never thought possible. Ariabella's wounds were healing and Cha loved having her as a pet. And then there was Etta and Sage.

She had mixed feelings. Even after Etta ran out on her and Sage, Cha felt sorry for Etta and missed her helping hands in the shop. Etta had taken advantage of Cha's trusting nature, even though Etta had given Cha her greatest gift, her son.

The morning after Etta left, Cha went through the motions to open her shop without any help, but closed early. There was much to be done, she didn't have a car, and she had to care for both Sage and Ariabella. When Etta had arrived, Cha wondered if the new arrangement would change her budding relationship with Rob in a negative way. Now with Etta gone and Rob's support, that part was of no concern. Her relationship with Rob became stronger and she knew it would continue to improve, no matter where Sage slept. *We're a team*, she reminded herself.

Given the circumstances of the previous night, Rob agreed to come by to help out. They worked out the particulars of Cha buying the cottage. Not only was it a relief to have that settled, she now had the added bonus of Rob's helping hands. In his attentive way, he brought out the best in her and he said she did the same for him. He posted her old rainbow-colored mailbox and helped her clean the kitchen before launching in on Sage's bed project. Rob showed Cha how Sage could have his own room by putting up two walls. His window would look out on Ariabella. Cha agreed the privacy would be welcome. She decided to give Sage a little time before enrolling him in school.

Cha was able to establish a rhythm where she woke, took care of Ariabella, and fixed Sage's breakfast before attending to her business. Rob was there for her every day, as he had been from the beginning. She knew he felt as she did, especially at night when Sage was asleep and they lay in each other's arms. Their conversations included long-range plans that spoke of continued commitment.

Rob had taken to Sage as quickly as Cha had when they first met. He proved to be a tender, yet strong force in Sage's life, and Sage looked to him for guidance, sometimes asking questions until his sleepy eyes could stay open no longer.

One evening after looking at the stars on a moonless night, Rob and Cha were helping Sage into his pajamas when he said, "My Etta taught me some good stuff about the stars. When we slept in parks or on the streets, my Etta and I did a lot of star watching."

Cha said, "Would you like for us to get a telescope? We can see the stars up close. Rob, doesn't Zarah have one? Let's ask her if we can borrow it."

"Rob," Sage said in a concerned voice. "I feel wrong."

"I know, Sage. It hasn't been that long since your mother left. It will take a while for you to feel better."

Rob gave him a hug and Sage wrapped his small arms around his leg.

"No, it's Ariabella," Sage said. "She needs us. She is afraid. A monster is trying to hurt her. Can we please check on her, Mr. Rob?"

Sage was upset and Cha had learned to trust his intuition. "Rob, will you please check on Ariabella? There is a flashlight on the table next to the side door." At that moment, the donkey brayed in distress, startling the two of them. "Hurry!"

Cha kept Sage close to her side as the two went to his window. She opened it to see what was going on.

Rob catapulted himself down the stairs and out the side door, picking up the flashlight on his way out. He ran toward the shed. The braying was nonstop. The flashlight cast a beam through the dark, illuminating a young boy standing at the shed.

"You there! What are you doing?"

Cha held Sage close as they watched from above.

The outer antique iron shed doors had not been latched. Rob had salvaged them from a torn down antebellum estate. She thought it possible the young man had come to steal them, but piercing cries were coming from the direction of Ariabella's stall. She could make out the sound of her hooves kicking the wood sides of the shed. *Aw-eeah! Aw-eeah!*

The boy put his hands in the air and shouted, "Help us! That donkey's crazy! I don't have a weapon. We didn't intend any harm, and my brother is in bad shape. That mean animal kicked him in the head. He's bleeding. The donkey tried to kill us!"

Rob stayed a short distance back and spoke to Ariabella. "It's okay, girl, calm down. Come here. Come on…"

Ariabella walked over to Rob and shielded him from the young men. Rob rubbed her head, trying to put her at ease. She was his first concern. Rob walked closer, shining the light in the intruder's eyes, with the donkey close to Rob's side.

Rob yelled, "Take that rope off the hook on the door and bring it to me. I'm warning you, if you try anything, this donkey is ill tempered. You have experienced a taste of what she can do."

The boy walked to Rob, causing Ariabella to dig her hooves into the ground. Rob tied the boy's hands behind him and secured him to a fence rail. "What are you doing here?" he demanded.

"We were looking for anything we could sell and thought the donkey would be worth some money. We need money, mister, to get away from Pa," the boy said.

"Everyone in town knows this animal. Not only is it wrong to steal, you would have been caught soon enough. It sounds like you're in a bad situation, but there are honest ways out, smarter ways where you won't get yourself hurt. You should have considered the danger before you committed a criminal act. Maybe you should talk with the good sheriff about the trouble with your Pa. Hmm?" The boy didn't answer.

Rob ran his hands along Ariabella's flanks. "It's all right, girl. Trouble's over. Come on out now." The donkey allowed Rob to lead her out of the shed.

The boy called out, pleading, "Mister, I'll do as you say, but please get help for my kid brother. I got him into this mess. He could bleed to death. Are you going to help him?"

"I'm going to call for a doctor."

Taking in everything from her perch, Cha said, "Sage, stay here. I need to go down and help."

Cha ran downstairs and met Rob by the side door where they secured the donkey. Cha went into the shed with Rob to check on the bruised and bleeding boy. Rob pulled off his shirt and pressed it onto the boy's wounded head. Cha could see that if Ariabella had struck a few inches lower, the boy's eye could have been destroyed.

"Cha," Rob said, "I'll stay here with this kid. Call Sheriff Curtis. Tell him what's happened, and that we need a doctor."

Cha went in and made the call. Sage came downstairs and joined her.

"Is Ariabella going to be okay?" he asked.

"Yes, Sage. We've had a bit of unwanted excitement, but she's fine. Ariabella is a fierce fighter, like you. You may have saved her by your power to know things. We are blessed you are with us. Now, go back upstairs. The sheriff will be here soon."

"Is the sheriff going to arrest my Etta?"

Cha held Sage and smoothed his hair from his forehead. She could see he was emotionally drained. His past, unstable life had prepared him to sort out most problems, but he was easily upset. "No, Sage. Your mother has moved on, that's all. Go on, now."

"I love you, Miss Cha."

"I love you, too, Sage."

It wasn't long before the sheriff arrived with his car lights flashing. He and a deputy stepped out.

"Sheriff." Rob greeted both men. "Two boys were trying to steal this animal and she kicked one of them in the head. He's bleeding, but he seems to be okay. I tied his older brother to the fence."

The men escorted the hurt teenager out into the open field. Rob held his flashlight while the sheriff looked him over. The deputy radioed for help. Within minutes, the paramedics arrived and administered to the boy. They took him to the hospital.

"Yeah," the sheriff said, "I know these two. They go around stealing and fencing other folks' property. No one will hire them. Their daddy is a violent drunk with his own rap sheet. I can't remember how many times I rescued those boys after their daddy beat them. They've lived a rough life. Maybe this encounter will literally knock some sense into them. It won't be easy, but they need to find a better way out of their chaotic life. They're young. There's hope for them yet."

Cha noticed how the sheriff's voice softened toward the boys.

"Maybe so," Rob said. "People can lose hope when they live under such extreme circumstances. Still, breaking the law is a risky way to go."

Sheriff Curtis cuffed the boy before he untied him. "Well Daryl, what do you have to say for yourself?"

"We didn't mean harm. It's just an old donkey," Daryl replied.

"Regardless, it's someone else's donkey. To them, she is a member of their family. What is it going to take to get some common sense into that head of yours? Your background is no excuse. This is wrong and you should know it. Is this how we welcome a new citizen to our beautiful town? Before I take you in, you're going to apologize to Miss Cha. It will be up to the lady to decide about pressing charges against the two of you."

"Sheriff," Cha said, "Do you have a rehabilitation program where these kids can get turned around?"

"Interesting you should say that. I was about to ask Rob; would you be interested in joining me and some other citizens in joining a planning committee? Our town needs a youth center and a work training program. We need to get out of the talking stage and start doing something."

"Sure. I always have ideas jumping around in my head." Rob gave a small laugh and said, "I'm good at most things. Zarah saw to that. Anytime, Sheriff Curtis."

They shook hands.

"Say 'hey' to Zarah for me." The sheriff finished with his notes.

Cha stepped inside her shop and returned with a box of muffins for the sheriff to pass around his department.

"Sheriff, thank you for your service. Please make sure these boys get some. It's a little reward for you, and I'd like to think an incentive for the boys to turn their lives around. I want them to know someone cares about them, even though they tried to steal from me."

Sheriff Curtis smiled and thanked Cha. He shook his head. "If only it were as easy as eating a turn-around muffin."

Daryl stood with his head down, his hands cuffed behind his back. The sheriff put his hand under the boy's chin. "Stand up and look Miss Cha in the face! Now let's hear what you have to say."

"I am truly sorry. If we can have another chance, my brother and I will work to repay any trouble we have caused. I am sorry."

Cha said, "Sheriff, I believe Daryl realizes his mistake, and not only because he got caught. I don't wish to see him in jail. We will talk about some public service for the two. I think these boys would do well in a program like the one you'd like to start."

"Goodnight. We'll be in touch." After putting Daryl in the back of his patrol car, the sheriff pulled away.

Rob returned Ariabella to her shed. She stubbornly dug her hooves into the grass. Rob cleaned out the blood-soaked straw, and then she went in without hesitation.

Cha went upstairs and once more reassured Sage while tucking him into his new bed. Cha told him it was okay to be afraid at times. Now, with their troubles over, they could all sleep well. "Rob and I are right here," Cha reminded him. "Just call if you need us."

"Miss Cha, will you say a prayer for my Etta? I miss my Etta, I don't believe she will ever come back. Why? My Etta always told me how much she loves me. I didn't understand all of my Etta's letter."

"Sage, I want you to get some rest. A lot has happened tonight. Tomorrow, we will spend the day together. You can help me in the shop. What do you think?"

"I would like it. I can help with the customers."

Cha thought, *how can this little boy express all he must feel and think about his mother? It's horrible, the emotional pain she put him through. Etta is his mother. That's just the way it is.*

Cha went downstairs and saw Rob had poured them two large apricot brandies. Neither was in the mood to talk. As Cha sipped her brandy, she thought about how Rob had walked into a chain of events that would dissuade most men.

"You are my knight in shining armor."

They hugged and he whispered in her ear, "And you are my queen."

She smiled. They took their drinks upstairs and showered. Both fell asleep exhausted.

Cha awakened at six with Rob at her side. She draped his arm over her and he pulled her in close. There were no words to describe how great it felt to be held and loved. Cha thought, *this is what being part of a couple is supposed to be like.* It felt perfect. She could have stayed wrapped in contentment, but managed to pull herself away. She dressed for the day, picking out special jewelry to wear. Without making a sound, she left the room to prepare her muffins and open the shop.

She had not heard Sage stir and though she assumed he was still asleep, she cracked the door to his room and saw his small form resting peacefully beneath his Superman sheets. There was no telling how long it would take for him to deal with Etta's abandonment. She would do her best to help him until he found peace. She thought about the pain Etta must have felt. Poor Etta had given up, but she loved Sage enough not to take him with her.

Raising the curtains, she saw Sheriff Curtis pull up in front of the shop. She poured two cups of coffee. She liked Sheriff Curtis. She would never forget it was he who introduced her to Rob that day in the diner.

Sheriff Curtis completed the reports on Ariabella and confirmed Cha did not wish to file complaints against the boys. "Miss Cha, I found work for the two boys. Let Rob know. I believe this time they will turn their life around. Maybe it was your muffins. My wife said I have been sweeter since eating them." He took a drink of his coffee and said with a big grin, "Something good is going on in Divine." He took Cha's hand and kissed it.

"You are too sweet! Thank you. Bring your wife and kids by some-time for some muffins and hot chocolate. I'd like to meet them."

"I thought I'd save the best news for last. I got a call this morn-ing from the Birmingham PD. Your car was towed from a parking lot behind a Greyhound station. There's nothing wrong with it. The keys were under the mat. I've got a couple of guys on their way to pick it up."

"Oh, that is the best news! I have missed Woody like you wouldn't believe."

"No sign of the woman. If you don't want to be found, better not drive a wagon everyone notices. I'd better go. You've got paying customers." She gave the sheriff a hearty handshake and he left.

Customers had entered the shop and she was not prepared. Cha set "Today's Special" sign out front and opened windows, airing the aromas of cinnamon, lemon, and vanilla with the mix of herbs and berries. She inhaled to let their healing qualities swirl inside her. The smells were intoxicating, and once passers-by took in the seductive aromas, they were hooked, too. She placed the herb muffins in open baskets on the wooden counter.

A smile spread across her face as she watched the citizens of Divine mingle on the streets. She liked the people of this town. Cha often got a chuckle when she stopped by the post office. Without lifting his head, Mr. Sands, the friendly postmaster, would say, "Afternoon, Cha. Lemon muffins on the menu today? You make my day, coming in here smelling like that shop of yours."

Cha's gently refined Southern voice and dainty laugh belied her formidable presence. Her height, once a source of frustration, felt natural, and now that she was on her own, she experimented by creating her own personal style. She wore her fiery, sunset red hair to suit her mood: down on one side, clipped up, in a ponytail, and on some days, she wove beads or colored ribbons into her braids. She enjoyed playing around with color and her style became as diverse as the menu in her quaint muffin shop.

She didn't think of herself as beautiful, though Rob told her this often. Her large eyes, she supposed, were her best feature. Their deep chocolate brown color added depth next to her vibrant hair. She noticed things many others missed, little details she would write in her notebook or squirrel away in her mind to ponder later.

Remaking herself was a process that would take time. She tried to remove all non-loving thoughts from her mind as they arose, choosing not to blame her parents or her past for any unhappiness. She took responsibility for her life and acted upon it. To remind herself, she looked at a note she had written the previous evening, something Sheriff Curtis had said to the boys she found poignant. The note said: "The statute of limitations has run out on continuing to blame your folks."

With no relations to call on, Cha spent time getting to know Zarah, who shared her interest in becoming friends, especially since it was apparent her son had chosen Cha as his special someone. Cha did not discuss her old family life with Zarah, though she suspected Zarah could tell there was a wheelbarrow full of hurt somewhere in her past. She thought to call Zarah and then she would wake Rob. As she reached for the phone, it rang.

"Cha's Muffin Shop."

"Cha, this is Zarah."

"I was just thinking about you! Nice to hear your voice. I am looking forward to the canoe trip—soon, I hope."

"Yes, dear, so am I. Sorry to trouble you so early. I need to speak with my son. I am not feeling well enough to drive to the doctor's. It may be my new medication."

"Do you want to hold, or should I send him to you right away?"

"Send him to me."

"I will give him some herbs for tea. Maybe they will help soothe you."

"You are a dear. I am going to be fine. And, another thing, tell him to bring an order of those famous muffins of yours. Goodbye."

Rob came into the kitchen. "Was that my mother?" Cha nodded. "Sounds like I'm on a mission. Don't know when I'll be back. Depends on how Mom is. Love you. You look beautiful this morning." He took the box of muffins and a packet of herbal calming tea and headed out.

Cha took care of her customers. Her ginger pumpkin muffins infused with herbs sold out and she hustled to keep the coffee going. Another popular item was the dinosaur muffin inspired by Sage's love of Dino. She positioned a toy dinosaur atop each fragrant muffin. A small scroll attached with a thread gave a brief description of the Brontosaurus, Pterodactyl, T. Rex, and Triceratops. The muffins were a hit with parents and children alike and the kids were fast becoming toy collectors.

When the shop cleared out, Cha went upstairs. She woke Sage, gave him some breakfast, and let him assist her with feeding Ariabella. Morning mist rose from the pasture. It felt good on her arms as she and Sage traipsed to the feed shed. Sage chattered away about the courage Rob and Ariabella had shown in the presence of the young toughs. Witnessing Sage's strength made Cha's spirit dance. She marveled at the miracle of his childhood and realized he would be a good example for her when she wanted to access her own childlike nature.

He asked about Etta. "Will the nice Sheriff look for my Etta and bring your car back?" Sage looked at Cha for reassurance.

Cha nodded and said, "My car will be back soon. Your mother needs some time away."

"Look, Miss Cha, the jonquils are starting to bloom along the fence. Do you think Ariabella will eat them?"

"No! She is a flower child. She might bring me a bunch."

"Do you like flowers that look like sunshine? I like them a lot! Can we plant more, Miss Cha, can we?"

Cha smiled. Somehow Sage's soul shone through the messes in their lives, even things hard for adults to handle. *Sage endures. He has remained a child of great hope with the ability to push sadness aside to enjoy the beauty of a yellow flower.*

"Yes, Sage, we will plant hundreds in this field, so many that when they burst into bloom, you will have to wear sunglasses!"

Sage laughed, and then got serious. "Miss Cha, tell me about when you were little. Did you help your mother plant flowers?"

Sage didn't always wait for answers. If you didn't respond fast enough, his mind and body were somewhere else. Sage ran ahead to open the shed door to let Ariabella out. The donkey nuzzled him, then waited for her food.

Cha admired the unique shed built from reclaimed wood. She loved the little touches like the small stained glass window that graced the back of the shed. *That's my Rob*, she thought, *he isn't just a builder, he is an artist of the highest order.*

After the donkey was fed and running in the pasture, Cha and Sage walked to the large sheltering tree and sat beneath its shade.

"Will you tell me a story about when you were little? First, may I give Ariabella some flowers for her harness? Maybe the yellow flowers will brighten her day, too. Those mean boys must have made her a little sad. I'll hurry back!"

Sage ran across the pasture and after putting the yellow jonquils in place, Ariabella shook and a few fell off. Cha thought about her parents having pleasing thoughts from the jonquils blooming around their resting place. Cha asked herself how much she should reveal to Rob and Sage of her life growing up on the tree farm. There were things that gave her happiness, like planting tree seedlings that would be easy to share.

"Sage, I helped my father in the garden and on our farm. My mother preferred to be inside. Dirt, insects, sweat bees, and sun all made her uncomfortable."

"Was your mother afraid of things outside? Did she get sad, like my Etta?"

"Mother was afraid of lots of things. I didn't understand my mother. I wasn't as wise as you are. My mother was beautiful, but I don't think I ever told her. Father taught me about nature and he loved plants, grew trees, and the greenest cedar trees a person ever saw."

Sage lost interest in Cha's recollections as he ran off to chase a butterfly.

"Let's go back in, Sage," Cha said. "I heard the bells. We have customers to help and muffins that need to come out of the oven."

Sage helped with customers for a while, but lost interest in favor of playing with Dino on the floor. He stayed where Cha could keep an eye on him and still run her business.

"My Cha! My Cha! I hear Rob's truck. May I go greet him? He likes me to greet him with big bear hugs."

"Go!"

Cha went to the side door. Rob walked up carrying Sage on his shoulders and they waved as they went by. Ariabella trotted up to greet the two of them. She was happy to see them. She bobbed her head and nuzzled them while making funny noises of approval. Sage petted her head. Rob set him down and Ariabella ran around the pasture with Sage running along beside her.

Cha came out and stretched her arms towards the clear sky. "I give thanks for this chance to share my stored-up love with this village, my muffin shop, Rob, Zarah, Sage, and the phenomenal Ariabella."

Rob, Sage, and the donkey joined her under the tree. Cha asked about Zarah, mentioning that she could tell something was out of character when they spoke on the phone. Rob said he was worried, he had never seen his mother heavy-hearted. "But, Mother assured me this illness has a lesson in it somewhere. Her doctor ordered some tests. She will take care of it."

Holding both her hands out to Rob, Cha said, "I had a neighbor friend growing up named Mr. Levy. He had a saying, 'Things will work themselves out, all in due time.' I believe he was right."

"Yes, I have no doubt Mr. Levy is right," said Rob as they watched Sage and Ariabella enjoy the freedom of the pasture.

CHAPTER NINETEEN

Loving Care

As the weeks unfolded, Cha was able to make her vision come true for the muffin shop, and the citizens of Divine helped make it a reality. They looked forward to picking up their muffins in the morning. Passers-by made a point of walking on the muffin shop side of the street where conversations would break out between those sitting at the outdoor tables. Cha returned their cheerful hellos. Ariabella and Sage often played close by in the field, and they received their share of visitors, too.

Cha asked for guidance each morning upon entering her eclectic, well-ordered kitchen. It paid off with happy, satisfied customers. Everyone seemed drawn to Cha's growing list of muffins, which she listed on an artistic, outdoor sandwich sign. As they reviewed her menu, folks would stop and chat about the inviting aromas drifting out the open windows.

Her regular offerings were: Carrot Pumpkin Raisin—for eyesight and to see interest in small everyday things, Sweet Potato with Sesame and Orange Zest—a mood lifter, Chocolate with Dark Red Cherries—for joint aches, Fig-Flax-Oat-Sweet Coconut—a morning wakeup cleanse, and Sunny Lemon Strawberry—for romance. She added seasonal options and took suggestions from her customers. Her offerings expanded with the introduction of Billy's honey and locally-sourced jams, which added to her growing profit. Soon she would invest in a professional-grade bread machine to add an array of healthy breads to the menu.

Visiting with customers outside gave her a chance to admire the exterior of the cottage. The sight made her smile. Rob found etched glass windows in an old abandoned inn, and when he showed them to her, Cha fell in love with their beauty. The following morning, Rob showed up at daybreak to install them. Rob painted the shop a sunny yellow with deep purple trim around the windows as Cha imagined. The front seating areas outside the cottage were fenced in and adorned with window boxes painted purple with yellow polka-dots. They overflowed with assorted blooming medicinal herbs. Rob's artistry complemented hers, and the townsfolk were attracted to the welcoming environment. A few of the older people in the town would sit for hours, reading the newspaper with a cup of coffee, or playing chess or checkers. Cha planted a couple of small trees in pots to give them shade.

She sewed tablecloths, using material found at a sidewalk sale. The material was perfect, featuring a light violet background scattered with dark red cherries. When she found this treasure, she had been tickled, but not surprised. When things were right, they fell into place. Everything happened for a reason.

The drinking bowls Cha placed outside for the animals encouraged people to stop by while walking their dogs. Stray cats soon found they were welcome, along with squirrels and friendly crows.

Cha often paused to look out the kitchen's new pop-out window to see Ariabella at play in the pasture. Her handsome head and large ears would tilt back as she happily brayed at the sky. Sage often ran alongside her, laughing at the donkey knocking around a soccer ball. These days her thick coat shone with health, reflecting the loving care she received. A purple and yellow ribbon was braided in her tail, and she wore a halter. Cha attached turquoise stones to old silver buckles and stitched them to the halter like jewelry.

Ariabella had become a major attraction. Adults and children visited daily. The little ones sat on the fence to extend greetings, loving pats, and the occasional apple. Sage played with these children, his new friends. Sage, who learned responsibility early in life, adored Ariabella. He took pleasure in caring for her and making sure she was groomed daily. The two were at ease with each other and showed affection often.

How our lives have changed, Cha thought. She expressed gratitude for the miracles in her life. Three damaged souls—Cha, Sage and Ariabella—had come together to find happiness, healing, and renewed spirit. Zarah assisted Cha in obtaining a family lawyer to resolve Sage's custody, and now Cha felt secure knowing her family was united emotionally and legally.

Cha, Rob, Sage, Ariabella, and now Zarah, were becoming a family. Zarah would often drop by Cha's shop to chat. Cha was all ears listening to Zarah's stories about her single life and being pregnant with Rob. Zarah described their early days as being filled with the search for adventure.

The three adults and Sage often got together for family discussions and to share their feelings. Cha opened up about her unhappy childhood. She wanted Sage to understand that even if things looked perfect on the outside, inside they could be less than cheery. She admitted that she didn't always think back kindly on the time when she had been forced to be a caretaker for her mother, especially during her teen years. She hadn't asked for the responsibility. Inside, she felt that one day her experiences would prove to be a benefit. She would run her own life as an adult and with luck, care for children. Ariabella was an unexpected bonus. She couldn't feel negative when her past experiences had brought her to this wonderful place in life that only seemed to get better with each passing day. Her happiness with Rob, so wonderful and unexpected, completed the picture.

Rob talked about his childhood and his interests in woodworking, which he was able to develop with the help of a family mentor. He tried to relate some of his experiences so Sage could find hope for the future. He complimented Sage on his strength and bravery, and reminded him how his mother loved and protected him. Sage could be grateful for those things and for the love other people brought into his young life. Each person agreed the harsh realities of life, combined with their good experiences, made them the people they had become.

Cha changed her mind about sending Sage to public school. She wanted to give him time to adapt to all the changes in his life. In a short time, he had come out of his protective shell. He had put on weight and had experienced a growth spurt. He read far above his age level and was highly gifted with other skills. After demonstrating responsibility with Ariabella and seeing his attraction to all animals, it was natural for Cha to take in the two stray kittens that showed up at the front of the cottage and stayed.

Rob spent some nights at the cabin with Zarah, who was unusually tired. Cha missed him on those evenings, as did Sage. Rob had changed the locks on the cottage doors the day Cha moved in. It wasn't long before he had his own set of keys.

After spending one night at the cabin, Rob arrived early at the cottage and let himself in. With Sage asleep, Cha and Rob spent some time together in the bedroom before thinking about breakfast. Cha dressed and they walked arm-in-arm down the stairs. Neither of them had to verbalize their feelings. One look at their glowing faces told a story of love and connection.

"See you and Sage tonight for dinner," Rob said. "I'll pick up a pizza."

Cha stood in the chill air as Rob left. She stretched upward, feeling the cool morning mist on her arms, and gave thanks in appreciation for the joy she felt, directing her thoughts toward God, or more often, to the universe. She opened Ariabella's shed door. The donkey followed her back to the muffin shop, went to the kitchen window, and waited patiently for Cha to open the window.

There the animal received her Good Morning muffin, specially prepared each day for her. A kiss on her head resulted in a raspy bray, followed by another from a tickle under her chin. Ariabella pulled her lips back, showing a smile of healthy teeth. Cha laughed at her antics.

Carrying the warmth of Rob's breakfast visit, Cha prepared her muffin sign for the day, drawing a Sunny Lemon Strawberry muffin. They had become Rob's favorite. She smiled as she drew a cupid on top of the sign, and then added a few hearts and shooting arrows. The message of romance came through. She gathered the strawberries and lemons from the refrigerator to mix up a batch and took out the packet of silver cupids to place atop each muffin when it cooled—a delightful flea market find. As she slid the filled trays into the oven, her thoughts drifted to romantic love, the kind she felt with Rob. It made her heart flutter with gladness. What once had been a childhood question upon seeing Rhett and Scarlett was now a feeling that filled her with a delirious sensation of romantic love fulfilled.

How odd that one moment her soul felt oneness with the world, and the next, a smell would evoke an old memory connected to questioning thoughts. The drying rosemary hanging in the kitchen brought her father and mother present. *How much am I like them? I'm efficient and methodical—good traits, I realize now. I'm tall and have their straight posture, and yes, their good looks! I wish I had known their inner feelings, but Father just went along each day and Mother withdrew into her illness.*

The ringing of the Tibetan bells brought her back to the present. A familiar voice said, "Afternoon, Cha!" It was the local pharmacist.

"Hello, Mr. Nettles. Your wife's order is ready."

"My family is hooked on your muffins. Don't care much for sweets myself," he said as he sat close to the front window.

"How about a fresh cup of coffee?"

Mr. Nettles had a far-away look in his eye. Cha felt a special kindness toward the pharmacist and sensed a longing in him. On impulse, she selected a saucer that had a beach scene with two sandpipers painted on it and placed Mr. Nettles' cup on it.

Mr. Nettles put three mounded spoonsful of sugar into his cup and stirred. He brought the cup close to his face to enjoy the strong aroma of the steaming coffee and took a drink. He paused before placing the cup back on the saucer.

"Sandpipers," he said. "May I lay claim to this cup and saucer, Miss Cha?"

"Yes, you may! You just gave me a great idea for my regular customers. Their very own cup and saucer will be kept on this shelf. And you, Mr. Nettles, will be first."

After three cups of sweet coffee, Mr. Nettles became chatty about all manner of things and people, including his customers, giving updates on their jobs, marriage status, health, and who was mad at whom in the village. Cha wasn't big on gossip as the other people were not there to counter the words spoken about them. At those moments, she got busy with her work. When he switched to speaking about his personal feelings and life, she placed his yellow box of muffins on the table, pulled a chair out, and sat beside him.

"Coffee is on me today, Mr. Nettles, and I placed a special muffin inside the box for you. It has a palm tree on it. You do like the ocean, don't you?" She touched his hand and she noticed his eyes—ocean blue.

Mr. Nettles said, "Do you know I dream of the ocean every day? I close my eyes and take a long walk, feeling the warm sand on my bare feet. I taste the saltwater, maybe pick up a handful of seaweed. Oh, you must think I'm a foolish man."

"Not at all." Cha walked over to her treasure shelf and picked up a large seashell, which she presented to him. "My gift to you. Is there any reason you can't take a trip to the ocean? What's holding you back?"

Mr. Nettles furrowed his brow in thought. "I'm not sure, Miss Cha. Would I miss the dreaming if I went?" He cocked his head, tipped his straw hat to Cha, and picked up his order. "I sure hope these muffins are not full of sugar," he said with a wink.

"Have a good day, Mr. Nettles. Dreaming holds a good place."

Cha breathed a sigh of contentment. She enjoyed getting to know the citizens of Divine, and more, she considered them her friends. *My fantasy conversations have come alive.* Two customers came in and Cha stood ready to serve them.

Sage followed behind. Dino's yellow head stuck out of his backpack. Sage spoke to the couple in the shop. "Hi, Mr. and Mrs. Hill, want to come and say hello to Ariabella?" He reached for Mr. Hill's hand before they had a chance to answer. "Here, Mrs. Hill," Sage said, "you can carry Dino. I will hold Mr. Hill's hand to the pasture."

"We only have time to pick up our muffins, dear. We have company coming," said Mrs. Hill. "I'm sure they will love dining on Miss Cha's muffins."

"I'll go with you to the pasture," Cha said, "but only for a short while. Remember, we need to spend time working on your lessons. Go ahead while I finish my business with the Hills."

Sage was cheerful and obsessive about learning new things. He had a great interest in people and animals, and was often torn between interacting with them and wanting to study. When Sage entered the pasture and did not see Ariabella, he checked inside her shed. There, her attention was focused on something in the straw. Sage's heart quickened, remembering the incident with the bad boys. He felt safe knowing Cha was on her way. The shed was shadowy. He reached for the small red flashlight hanging low on a hook Rob had put there for him.

"My Cha! Come look!"

A ray of light shone on a large bird in the shed. Sage crept up to the frightened-looking bird. In his sweet voice, he said, "Hi there, don't be afraid; we will take care of you."

Cha came to the shed door and saw Sage sitting close to the bird. The bird, a type of parrot, appeared dazed. The bird took a short hop into a beam of sunlight that came through a crack in the shed. The extra light exposed more clearly the bird's raw, oozing exposed flesh. Its feathers were burned and it did not try to defend itself. Sage kept up a soft chatter, "I am going to wrap you in my shirt. What's your name? God will punish whoever let this happen. I love you. I am sorry you are hurt."

He gently put his small yellow shirt around the bird. Cha watched as Sage's tiny hands picked up the huge macaw. She trusted him with the hurt bird while wondering what they would do for it. The bird did not peck or resist Sage's help.

Ariabella stood close by. She gave Sage a nudge and sniffed the bird. Sage kissed her nose and said, "Thanks. The hurt bird lived through the night because you watched over it. I'll be back to groom you." The bird stayed motionless as Sage cradled it in his arms. "My Cha will heal your wounds."

"We will see what we can do," Cha said. "Take it inside."

The two walked back toward the cottage with the donkey right behind. She lifted her curious head to get a better look as they left her behind in the pasture.

In the bright light of day, Cha could see the bird's colorful head and beak, and wondered how the bird had come to be in its present state. She opened the side door. "Put the bird on the table and keep talking to it."

Sage did as Cha instructed. Tears streamed down his face as he saw the burned skin on the injured bird.

Cha proceeded to fill a small tub with warm water, baby shampoo, and her special healing salve. She administered loving care, removing bits of stuck-on straw and examined the extent of the bird's injuries. When she was done, she wasn't sure what to do next, but then remembered the antique birdcage. Once more, not knowing why she would purchase a seemingly random item only to find it would turn out to be exactly what she needed. She gave Sage directions to clean it out and line it with newspaper.

Sage decided to call the bird Tootsie. The poor thing was very sick, and Cha kept a close eye on her. She applied the salve several times a day. After a few weeks, Tootsie's burns healed over and she became very active. She thrived with love from her new family. Her long saber-shaped tail started to fill in with bright plumage, though her curved, powerful bill still showed scars.

Cha reported finding a large macaw to Sheriff Curtis. He posted a sign in town. Not surprisingly, he told Cha, "No one came forward to claim her."

As with the other creatures that came Cha's way, Tootsie became a part of the family. Sage put two small bells around her neck and Cha clipped her wings to make sure Tootsie stayed in close. Tootsie continued to improve and started talking nonstop. She had a unique stutter. Her preferred game was to take Cha's favorite foil-wrapped candies and hide them throughout the house and shop. She didn't eat the sweets, but Sage did when he found them. The two kittens were not as happy as the others with the new family member, but Sage said, "They will come to love Tootsie." And they did.

Sage told Cha, "Tootsie is happy now. She said she was treated so badly by her owner, that it's too painful for her to talk about it. But I hope Tootsie will tell us one day. But I understand why Tootsie won't talk about bad stuff. Do you, my Cha? You said bad things happened when you were young and you didn't have anyone to talk to."

"Yes, Sage. My childhood wasn't the happiest. My parents didn't do things on purpose to hurt my heart. Those days are over. God opened a new door for me, for you, for Ariabella, and Tootsie. Our tomorrows will be beautiful and our spirits will continue to soar."

"My Cha, I cried sometimes because my Etta and I slept on the street. She would hold me tight and promise me the morning would be a new beginning. Yes, she promised to try very hard to do better. My Etta did try."

Sage broke down and emotion shook his small body. Cha let him get the pain out. When he had calmed, Cha hugged him and said, "Your mother loved you deeply. This you know, you were a shining star in her life. Etta had been wounded from childhood. It made it hard for her to help anyone, but she tried, Sage. We must always remember there is a rainbow on the horizon."

CHAPTER TWENTY

Family Life

After Sage was tucked in for the night, Rob built a fire in the old stone fireplace he had restored. He told Cha about Zarah's diagnosis—leukemia. Cha poured two brandies.

"Rob, I know how hard it is when a loved one is going through hard times. I want to share Zarah's health issues in any way I can. I know little about cancer, but I know a lot about healing."

Rob sipped his brandy, but swallowed hard. "Zarah's leukemia involves the blood and she'll be treated for her particular kind of cancer. The cancer cells can get into the bloodstream and grow. They replace normal tissue."

"Do they know how bad it is?"

"Fortunately, it hasn't metastasized. The doctor said cancer grows at different rates and Zarah has a good chance. Besides you and me, Zarah has a good support system and some of them have experience with this. She will try vitamins, herbs, acupuncture, and standard medicine. She won't delay medical treatments. She begins chemotherapy next week."

Cha started to cry. "I believe with all my soul Zarah will survive this. Does she know you are sharing her illness with me?"

"Yes. She told me to tell you. She understands you are the woman in my life—forever. I won't hold anything back."

They sipped brandy until the fire reduced to embers. They cuddled, feeling their shared love, but also carrying heavy hearts out of concern for Zarah.

Rob awoke early so he could drive back to the cabin to check on his mother. Before he left, he asked Cha, "Why don't you, Sage, Ariabella, and Tootsie come to Zarah's for the weekend? Zarah would be delighted, and she wants to spend time with you all. I want you to see the floor to ceiling windows I salvaged from the old train station—all installed in Zarah's room. She loves the light and beauty."

Rob pulled Cha close. He slid his hand along her arm from her shoulder down to her hand, which he kissed. "Good hands, long, sharply defined, and strong with a sexy touch," he said. They shared a silent gaze and he was off. The soft Tibetan prayer bells chimed their song as Rob left.

Cha savored the sweetness of the moment. She still felt Rob's hand on her arm, his kiss on her hand, and his words in her thoughts. While getting dressed, she hummed to herself in the early morning semi-darkness of the apartment. Cha closed her eyes and thought of the tranquility and excitement Rob brought to her life.

Morning light drifted through the new skylights Rob had recently installed. Sage was sound asleep with the kittens curled up at his head. Tootsie slept in her new, large cage. Feeling full of love, Cha sat down and wrote some quick notes to the Levy family, and Billy and Annie, bringing them up to date on her life. They had kept in touch, writing about their joy and asking about hers.

Cha left Tootsie's cage covered. When Sage awakened, he would take care of Tootsie and Ariabella. Cha hoped her stubborn pet would not pull one of her defiant stand-offs over the weekend and not get out of her trailer. Oh well, she had slept in it before. Cha went downstairs to open the shop.

She heard Tootsie talking in her funny little stutter. "S-s-sun's out, dar-dar-darlings. Tootsie needs to get up." Cha laughed. The shop was busy that day. Cha posted a notice to inform her clientele the shop would be closed on the weekend in case anyone wanted to purchase extra muffins.

During a break, she paused to look at her latest art addition—a fallen tree limb she had hung from the high ceiling. She adorned it with her newly begun collection of colorful glass items, brown globes, stars, and a small stained glass window. Some were gifts from Rob and Zarah. A large blown glass flower hung in the center, it's bloom facing down where she could see it—a gift from Sheriff Curtis thanking her for helping to cure his wife's persistent rash. Cha had mixed a concoction of herbs and essences in Special Breakfast muffins and had created a salve. The sheriff was delighted when his wife's skin cleared up.

The weather had been rainy off and on the entire week. Homes along the river had been put on flood alert as the river rose. Rob called to say the road was okay to travel. Cha looked forward to the weekend. She hoped her knowledge of healing herbs and essences would be able to ease and improve Zarah's health in her fight against the terrifying diagnosis.

Cha looked forward to spending time with Zarah in her charming home. The house was built with unusually handsome detail, created with Rob's artistic eye. Zarah added to the environment with a style of decorating that felt like strong magic to Cha. Containers of overflowing wildflowers, both fresh and dried, hung in baskets on doors and were strung across windowpanes. Intricately shaped branches from pines, dogwood, and sourwoods combined with ceramic pottery to create a pleasing decor.

Rob turned the truck radio to his favorite bluegrass station as he navigated the isolated road home. His growing distress over Zarah's recent medical reports from her doctors filled his head. He couldn't even begin to think of a life without his mother's effervescence. She had always been there for him in a loving, compassionate way, which imparted magic and hope to his world. But Rob knew, as Zarah had taught him, there comes a time when life brings sorrow. It's only a matter of when. He was also taught to believe in happy endings.

Zarah slept more, a far cry from her customary behavior. Memories of her extraordinary spirit came to mind. He could not think of a time when she showed lack of courage. She understood people's weaknesses. She pushed Rob to seek truth in life, and then do what was right. He said a quiet prayer to be there for her, "God, give me the courage I will need, if I have to say goodbye to Zarah." How could this be? He always felt Zarah was indestructible.

Rob missed the excitement of Zarah's friends. He never knew who would be their house guest. It could be the couple who owned the hardware store who lost their home, or another person who needed support for a short time. There was the woman she met on a rock and gem expedition in Australia, the hardworking waitress at the truck stop who lost her job and needed a place to stay until she got back on her feet, or that track star from Kenya who made his way through their area. The list went on and on.

His thoughts drifted back to Cha and how he was revealing more of himself to her. He told Cha he never missed having a father. He carried no longings from his childhood. "Mother never wanted me to be in a position of not being in charge of my life, and she set the highest standard for me to strive for as a human being. She is delighted about us."

As he pulled into the gravel drive, he spotted a barn owl on the front porch rail. The owl looked at ease and Rob thought the dogs must be in the house with his mother. They rarely left her side.

Rob sat in the truck, not wanting to disturb the seldom seen owl. He could see the glow of a fire coming from inside and was reminded of when he placed the stones to build the fireplace. As a boy, there had been many happy days as he and his mother canoed the river searching for stones while having long talks about life. Zarah photographed the many animals they would come upon. He would holler, "Look at this perfect stone, and over there, by that tree, a deer!" She made him feel exceptional.

He thought back to when she sent him to live the summer on a remote Native reservation to learn about the people's oneness with the earth, connecting the spirit to each element of nature, and to know how to live and survive in extreme social conditions other than his own environment. At first, he missed his mother and the river, but his adventures built his character into a well-rounded person.

After exiting the truck, he circled the house to the side porch. Zarah had turned it into a haven for herself with a large worktable for her gem cutting and jewelry making. Since her illness, she now slept in a bed on the porch when weather permitted. A mattress was put down on the stone floor for the dogs. Rob approached without making a sound, hoping the barn owl would stay around long enough for him to show his mother. He gave a soft known whistle to signal the dogs he was approaching. He didn't want them barking.

Zarah awoke. "Hi, son. Not an active day for me. Sorry, I had to ask you to come home. How did Cha take the news of my illness?"

"Extremely hard. But she was glad you wanted to share it with her."

"She's my kind of person."

"Mother, put on a sweater and come out the back door. I want to show you an amazing sight." Rob noticed how frail she appeared, whereas a few days ago, she felt well enough to split firewood. He put his arm around her as they rounded the corner of the cabin. He understood how hard it was for her to need someone.

Both froze in wonder as the white, golden-tipped barn owl spread its splendid wings and lifted off only inches from their heads. They could hear the swish of its wings as it continued down the river. Mother and son stood in awe.

"Thanks," Zarah said. They walked back to the house. "All of a sudden I have a craving for a huge meal of pancakes, cheese grits, and champagne! Good food always lifts me up."

Rob had not let his emotions get to him since his mother's diagnosis. He felt her spirit and determination could pull her through anything, so why not this? Overcome in her presence, he gave in to his grief and his body rattled deep inside with racking sobs. She put her hand on his arm and led him to the old, worn, brown leather chair where he could take comfort by the fire. He sank into it…this same chair in which she had confronted and explained life questions to him as he grew up. Her protective love hadn't stopped when he was no longer a child.

"Mother, you have been a never-ending inspiration for me, teaching me to reach out to grasp meaning instead of merely existing. You were so good about exposing me to great novels, biographies of people who followed their hearts with music, art, and different cultures. You helped me respect all life, people, animals, and nature. And now, I have found a unique woman I treasure with all my heart. I want you to know it's because of you. You were my role model and that is why I appreciate how wonderful Cha is."

"It's okay to get out your feelings. I know you are worried about me and are fearful that I won't be around much longer. I have a lot of living to do, and Cha and I have much to experience now that I know her. I believe the owl brought us a message of renewed hope. Now, let's eat our food and plan for our future. It would be nice to go canoeing on the river this weekend. Even though the water is up, we have challenged that old river lots of times. What time are we expecting Cha to arrive?"

"She will be here early evening. I hitched Ariabella's trailer to the woody for her, so she's ready to go."

After Cha had finished setting up the shop and putting the bread and muffins in to bake, she went upstairs to check on Sage. He was dressed and cleaning Tootsie's cage. Tootsie was perched on a swing Rob made for her, chattering away with her sweet stuttering. "Good-goo-good morning Mee-mee Cee." Cha gave Tootsie's feathers a ruffle and gave her a kiss on the beak. Tootsie's whimsical personality put a smile on the face of anyone who met her. *Tootsie was meant to be a part of this family*, Cha thought.

Sage smiled and said, "My Cha, it sure smells good. What special muffins are you making today? Some friends came to watch Ariabella. May I take some to them? I taught her some new tricks. She's a star!"

"I will put some in a sunny yellow box. Your friends will like them."

Sage helped pick out some muffins. He recited one of his rhymes, "I'll be back quick as you can say, 'Ariabella runs real fast, but then she stops for a bite of grass.'" He ran out the side door into the pasture where his friends waited. Cha thought, *how wonderful to see Sage being a silly kid.*

Sage returned with a large wildflower bouquet. Cha smiled and said, "Very pretty."

"I picked them for Zarah. Will she like them?" Sage brimmed with delight. "My Cha, if a small flower makes you smile, a big bouquet should give Zarah a big laugh. Oh, did you notice I am getting taller? I can almost reach Ariabella's head to put her lead rope on her without leaning down."

"Yes! I noticed your socks are showing below your pants. Next week, we'll make a shopping trip for new clothes." Cha gave him a hug and said, "Now off with you. Have fun. Don't work Ariabella too hard. Tonight, she will be anxious at Zarah's. We don't want her to be awake all night braying. With so much going on, she feels a little neglected these days. Give her a good grooming, including a bath."

"Thanks, my Cha." Sage ran off.

Cha marveled at the great job Sage did at taking care of the animals. He loved them so much. He took good care of his own space, too, keeping it very organized. Cha never had to tell Sage to pick up his clothes or put any of his toys away. His growing collection of dinosaurs was placed around his bed, each one in its own special place. Before bedtime, Sage cleaned his shoes, and put away his books and board games. He would then say his own special prayer, giving thanks for each person, animal, flower, and tree. His wisdom and sense of duty went beyond his years. Sage had thanked Rob many times for the storage space under his enclosed bed. Sage treasured any small gift given him. Cha's heartfelt love and admiration for the young boy grew stronger each day.

Cha heard the timers go off for the muffins and breads, bringing her back to the present. She tended each customer with interest, asking about their lives and giving the ones with particular needs a small gift from her treasure shelf collection—a small doll, a book of poems, bell or whistle—always the right item to lift a spirit. Cha wanted her patrons to experience more joy and surprises than they expected when coming to her shop.

In between customers, she prepared fresh herbs from the garden for baking bread and muffins to take to Zarah. She never failed to give thanks to her father for giving her the appreciation of the various herbs... rosemary, thyme, or whatever was fresh waiting to be picked. He had been a patient teacher.

Cha laid out Sage's lessons for math and English, which he completed upon his return from play. Cha checked over his work. "Very nice! You have been studying. Now let's prepare for a great visit at Zarah's."

Cha called Zarah and asked if she needed anything.

"Rob is preparing dinner," Zarah said. "Just watch the road for deer. Also, the beavers are building new homes along the river and are back and forth across the road. See you soon."

Zarah sounded in great spirits. Cha was delighted with their growing friendship. Zarah had so many admirable qualities; she was independent, successful, kind, generous of knowledge, and most important, she controlled her world.

Cha made a large banana pudding piled high with three-inch meringue, and an assortment of breads that she packed into Woody, along with everything else for the weekend trip, including the animals and the things they would need. Seeing the packed-up station wagon reminded her of the road trip to Divine, except now, a local sign painter had lettered "Cha's Muffin Shop" on the side doors of the woody.

Cha and Sage got a late start, but driving under a sky with many stars and a silver moon captivated them. As they passed large trees, the light cast a mysterious scene of flickering shadows.

"My Cha, the shadows look scary and frighten me. Do you think Ariabella is afraid also?" Sage hugged his kittens closer inside his jacket, along with Dino.

"Sage, the trees are doing their moon dance for us. Remember when we did the hand shadows on the wall?"

"Okay, my Cha, we are not afraid anymore. Well, maybe a little bit. It takes time for being scared to leave, even if I understand the reason. I told our cats, Calico and Beau."

Cha turned the radio on. Patsy Cline was singing, *I Love You Honey*. Cha and Sage sang along.

"My Cha, I like singing. It makes me happy inside; my legs start moving. Maybe Tootsie and Ariabella are dancing." Sage started to laugh. "That's funny, thinking of a donkey and a bird dancing. My Cha, can we buy a record player? I will do more chores. Don't you think it would be good to play our own music? Tootsie bobs her head when she hears music."

"That's an excellent idea! After our weekend at Zarah's, we will put a record player on the top of our list. Sage, are you getting sleepy? Your head just bobbed, or was that to the music?"

Sage laughed, "A little, but I want to stay awake."

Within minutes, Sage was asleep and Cha turned the radio off. The drive to Zarah's ran along the river and Cha kept her eyes on the road. With the radio off, she noticed Ariabella was making a fuss in her trailer.

Sage woke, "My Cha!"

"Sage, are you okay?"

"I dreamed about my Etta. She was in the river. I don't think Etta is coming back. Something bad happened."

Cha knew Sage must wonder about his mother, even though he had spoken less about her as time passed.

"Sage, you can always talk with me about your mother. She loved you very much. Knowing she was ill and couldn't take care of you properly, she made the ultimate decision to see that you had a safe, loving home. She saw how happy you were here with me."

"I know. My Etta told me God sent you and Ariabella to love and protect me. My Etta was very, very sick. I tried to take care of her. God told me he took my Etta to be with him because God is the strongest and only he could protect her and give her a warm place to rest. I miss my Etta sometimes. She could tell good stories and cheer me up. Etta tried to be good."

"Sage, you are very wise." Cha reached over and held his tiny hand.

Cha steered Woody off the paved road onto the bumpy graveled drive. Ariabella, feeling the jolt, sounded her disapproval. Sparkling lights lit the remarkable floor to ceiling windows Rob had told her about, and Chinese lanterns filled the yard and porches. It was beautiful. Cha instructed Sage to put Calico and Beau in their crate until they could be introduced to Ruby, Lady, and Motoo.

The dogs ran out to meet them. Rob and Zarah were right behind. Rob looked handsome in his light brown suede shirt, jeans, and bare feet. Zarah wore a purple satin scarf, white flowing pants, and a black turtleneck sweater. She was dazzling despite her dire circumstances.

Sage jumped from the woody and ran to Rob. Rob lifted him high in the air. "Good to see you, buddy. I need some help around here and you're the guy." Sage laughed.

Zarah knelt to receive a bear hug from Sage. "I love you, Miss Zarah. God told me last night, when I said my prayers, you were getting well. It was an express prayer. Ariabella and I picked these flowers for you."

"An express prayer? Do tell," she chuckled.

"Miss Zarah, a person can't ask too often for things, but for a real big problem, God lets us send for fast results." His little face shone.

She held his hand, and said, "Thank you for the happy wildflowers, and your request to God on my behalf. I believe He heard you. I am feeling better and more hopeful. A messenger came today with hope."

"Miss Zarah, tell me, who was the messenger? Was it a person or an animal? How big?" Sage's curiosity had him jumping in his shoes.

"Tomorrow, Sage, when we have time, I'll tell you about the messenger. Can you contain your excitement until then?"

"Yes, Miss Zarah," Sage replied. "Do you want to help us get Ariabella from her trailer? She's nervous. I told her everything was going to be okay. It's just a different house, but she doesn't like dogs much. One ran into the pasture and nipped at her legs, but Miss Zarah, she can be tough. She kicked it. That poor dog never came back. Miss Zarah, my Cha said for my birthday we may get another donkey so Ariabella won't be so lonely when we can't be with her."

"I see," Zarah said.

Rob put the donkey in a roped off area in the barn, close to the house. Cha unloaded Woody, getting Calico, Beau, and Tootsie inside the welcoming cabin. It smelled of light, fresh wood smoke from the fireplace. A group of candles flickered on the porch.

Cha put her belongings in a room where she could see the river. It had windows on three walls that went from ceiling to floor and featured a small open patio outside. Sage was in a small connecting room with Tootsie and the two kittens. As she unpacked, Cha thought, *this is what family is supposed to be about, realizing how we need each other while honoring the freedom to be ourselves.*

Zarah's cat, Motoo, was not happy with the many animals and people invading his home. He hissed at the intruders and slinked around to stay aware of their movements.

"Cats decide on their own terms," said Zarah.

Cha's heart overflowed with love. She caught her reflection in the mirror. "Maybe a little too much jewelry," she laughed, "but I feel generous with myself today."

She turned out the light and readied to leave the room when she felt Rob's familiar touch. He turned her around to face him. "Cha, get used to me showing up, because from now on I will never be far away." The bedroom was dark except for the moonlight shining through the windows. The atmosphere was sensual; Rob's hand felt warm on her wrist. They kissed. "Let's join the brood," he said. "Later, we can put the dogs in the barn with Ariabella tonight so she won't be lonely."

Cha said, "I feel scared. Sometimes everything feels too perfect. We all miss you the moment you leave. You are my first man, and maybe my last. I want to be with you always. You know I am committed to us—forever. I want to marry you."

Cha's face flushed at her boldness, but she also felt proud. She had made a promise to herself to never hold back her feelings. Rob kissed her and though she felt her answer, she wanted to hear him speak it. It occurred to her that he might be the one who wanted to do the asking, but she had beat him to it and there was no taking it back. Before Rob could reply, Zarah and Sage walked up and he held his thoughts.

Zarah said to Cha, "May I call you by the name Sage has given you, 'my Cha?' Seems to fit. I like the sound of it."

"I like it, too."

The dogs ran up to give them wet kisses. Zarah said to the dogs, "Go keep Ariabella company. She is our guest, girls." Zarah gave them more praise and shooed Ruby and Lady off to the barn.

Sage washed up and all sat down to a dinner of local trout, beer for the adults, salad, and later, Cha's banana pudding and coffee.

Zarah said, "There is something special about a spectacular dessert that fulfills childhood dreams. I love it. Kudos to you, Cha."

All were in high spirits, though Zarah's fatigue waxed and waned. The most fun was watching Sage's happiness highlighted by Tootsie, who had escaped her cage and lit in the middle of the table. "Yes, yee yay! Tootsie's par-par-party." Tootsie flew over to Sage, landing on his shoulder, her talons almost knocking him out of his chair.

Cha noticed a wire band tied around Tootsie's leg with a rolled piece of paper attached to it. "What's this?" Cha asked.

Sage untied the wire and removed the note. Everyone was quiet, wanting to hear the message. Sage unrolled the note, "It's for you, my Cha. Do you want me to read it?"

"Yes."

In his small, but excited voice he read, "My dearest Cha, I do! I do!"

Cha put Rob's hand in hers and said to him, "There was a void in my world and I came to Divine to fill it. Your love has made my life complete. I love you with all that I am." Tears rolled down her cheeks. "These are happy tears. Now, let's all go for a walk by the river while we still can and talk about a wedding."

Rob took Cha into his arms and whispered words that made her smile.

CHAPTER TWENTY-ONE

Foreboding River

With lanterns in hand, they walked along a well-worn trail, keeping a safe distance back from the river's edge. The rushing waters could cave in the riverbank and send a person into the river. Cha and Rob walked ahead. Zarah's stamina wavered and Sage was happy to wait with her as she rested.

Zarah enjoyed Sage's kind nature and relentless curiosity. He asked questions nonstop, and then, a crushing sadness would come over him.

Zarah said, "Sage, let's sit here on these large flat rocks and talk about you."

His perfect little face tightened. Zarah sensed he worked hard to cope with the memory-laden baggage from his unstable mother.

"I don't always know why I feel sad, Zarah. May I call you Aunt Zarah? I have never had an aunt."

Zarah pulled him close and said, "It's a great honor for me to be your aunt. Now just talk; let out whatever comes loose. You will not be judged, dear Sage, you are a wonderful child." Zarah reached out and mussed his tight blond curls.

With trembling lips, Sage said, "I am happy, Aunt Zarah, with my Cha, Ariabella, and Rob. But sometimes I do feel blue."

"Of course, you do. It's natural to feel sad after a loss, especially of one's mother."

"Aunt Zarah, I'm not mad at my Etta for leaving me. I like being safe in a house with my Cha. When I slept on the streets with my mother I got cold, and I was afraid a rat would bite me. A rat bit Etta on her finger. Don't you think being bitten by a rat is scary, Aunt Zarah?"

"Yes, I do, and I believe you were very brave."

"I get the shivers sometimes, even when I'm not cold. But I liked being under the stars. My Etta pointed out constellations. We learned them from a book." Sage stood. "Maybe I will ask Santa for a tent, and we can camp by the river. I will point out the constellations to you. I need to study more about the stars and planets."

"That sounds like a great idea, Sage. I will look forward to it."

A stirring in the nearby grass caught their attention. "Listen!" Zarah reached for Sage's hand. "Be still so we don't scare it away."

At that moment, a red fox leaped into the air with a graceful bowed back. The fox danced around. Sage was beside himself with joy and interest until the fox emerged with a small mouse in its mouth.

"Aunt Zarah," he cried, "please save the mouse!"

Zarah turned to Sage. "No, it isn't always pretty, but necessary. It's part of the cycle of life. Do you understand, Sage?"

"Yes, Aunt Zarah, but it does make me upset." Sage covered his eyes with his hands, "Please, Aunt Zarah, tell me when the fox has gone."

At the sound of their voices, the fox darted away with its dinner. Zarah noticed the river had risen. "Come, Sage, let's walk fast." Sage held Zarah's hand and the two left the mounting danger of the river.

When they reached the house, Rob and Cha were busy hitching up the donkey's trailer. Tootsie was placed in her cage, and the two kittens were crated. In the distance, a flash of lightning lit the sky, followed by the distant roll of thunder.

Zarah called out to Rob, "Is Motoo in the house? He was around the barn when we left."

"Yes, Mother, I put her inside."

Cha said to Rob, "You look worried."

"The radio says bad storms are moving in. You saw the river. It's rising because it's raining upstream and could overflow. We all need to leave. I don't want to take a chance of the house becoming flooded, and the bridge could wash away. Mother and I rebuilt once before. If you are okay with her staying at your place until the water level drops, it would set my mind at ease. Or we can stay in the village with a friend."

Cha said, "I insist we all stay together. We are a family."

Zarah said, "Sounds like it's been decided, but I can't leave my pets here."

Thunder rumbled through the sky. Sage came running. "My Cha! Ariabella is in the barn shaking. She is scared of thunder, but she won't come out of the barn."

Cha said, "We will be with her shortly. Go help Zarah pack a few things. She will be staying with us tonight. We'll all be leaving soon."

The rain came fast. Rob and Cha donned yellow slickers and put Ariabella in the trailer. With little forethought, they were able to secure all the animals, putting the dogs in Rob's truck and Tootsie in the trailer. The cats rode in their carriers with Rob and Sage in the woody, while Zarah went with Cha in Rob's truck.

"Stay calm," Rob advised Cha. "I know the roads, so I'll head out first. Stay within sight of the trailer in case the road is washed out or there are any mishaps."

The drive back to the shop was both unnerving and energizing for Cha. The river was starting to claim the road. Rob drove carefully and Cha paced herself to stay a close, but safe distance. Cha felt secure knowing he was in front of her, and glad that Sage was with him. She was confident he wouldn't put the family in danger.

On arrival at the cottage, Rob escorted his loved ones inside before putting Ariabella in her shed. He hung his small radio there, leaving music playing and talking to her all the while, "I will be back to check on you before I go to sleep." He patted her flanks and felt her body jerk. A big crack of lightning lit up the pasture. She seemed okay with Rob there, but he couldn't stay with her all night.

Inside the cottage, Rob changed into clean dry clothes and sat down with his family in the crowded cozy home of his future wife.

Sage said, "Rob, Ariabella is afraid of lightning. May I go and sleep with her?"

Rob motioned for Sage to sit on his lap. "Ariabella will be okay. She's been through lightning storms before—like us." Later in the evening, Rob checked on her. Though unhappy, she was fine.

Rob was more concerned about how Zarah would take it if their home sustained flooding from the foreboding river.

"Rob, let's leave it to the will of the river. If it takes all we own, so be it. We will move into a new chapter. I never lived on the safe side of the mountain, but if circumstances change, there is another path to explore. As with everything, I will carry on. Remember I have Sage sending his express prayers." She smiled.

The storm tapered off by midnight and in the morning, Cha's crowded cottage was filled with an abundance of love with everyone happy to pitch in. The next few days were a time of adjustment. Motoo and the kittens became friends, and Tootsie's sweet soul cheered everyone. Aria settled in to her routine. The dogs loved the pasture and were building a protective bond with Ariabella and Sage. Cha also formed a bond with Lady and Ruby, believing that if she had been allowed to have a dog growing up, she would not have had the overwhelming loneliness she bore from year to year.

Zarah had renewed hope of beating leukemia. She enjoyed her new-found role within the cottage sharing chores with Cha and teaching Sage. This new lifestyle gave her a different way to express herself, to cultivate life in a busy home.

Zarah would smile hearing Sage's questions, such as, "How do I not think about things? Do people believe I'm weird because I talk to animals and understand them? How do I know who to trust?" His curiosity was endless, as her son's had been.

Rob loved playing with Sage, who had never hit a ball or been on roller skates. It gave Sage a chance to be a kid without the burden of responsibility he carried with his mother, and Rob had fun being a kid with him. He also gave Sage helper chores while teaching him how to build and be trustworthy.

Washed out roads meant travel was still limited. The muffin shop became a meeting place for locals to check up on their neighbors to see who was in need of what. The Divine citizens cared about their community and Zarah found herself joining those conversations. She made new bonds with the townsfolk, including Sheriff Curtis who stopped by to say the road to her house was safe for travel. Upon inspection, he found the water had not reached the cabin.

"Do you want to visit the house?" Rob asked.

"Yes," she said, "but no hurry. Even with no damage to the cabin or the land, I'd like to stay a while longer here if Cha is okay with that."

"You're thinking of joining us here in town, aren't you?" Zarah nodded. "Mother, I believe a change is long overdue. How about converting the old bank building? I always imagined it would make an intimate inn. It would keep you busy. I could do wonders with it. Remember all those old beams and the interesting windows? We could leave the stone walls. Just a thought."

"Sounds interesting," said Zarah.

Cha walked in, beaming with curiosity. "What's going on? Anyone up for a party tonight out under the pasture tree? Let's include all our animals. Plus, I also have a surprise to announce."

Zarah said, "Count me in, and Cha, I am going to be your new neighbor, down the street."

"Yes! Each day gets more beautiful."

"I should get going," Rob said. "All this rain damage has been keeping me busy. Today I'm repairing Mr. Nettle's drive and porch. Our good sheriff has been picking up Mr. Nettles each day to open the drugstore. Don't start the party without us. And besides, I hope to have a surprise, too," Rob said.

Sage walked in from feeding and brushing Ariabella.

"Hey buddy, want to help build the Nettles' porch? Could use you."

"Sure do!" Sage said. "I like to help people. Let me get my toolbox." Sage ran to the back porch and picked up his red toolbox with his name on it, kissed Cha and Zarah, and then put his hand in Rob's. Lady and Ruby were waiting by the door, anxious to ride along.

"Ready? Rob, I like Mr. Nettles. He likes the ocean."

"How do you know?"

"The big seashell was gone from my Cha's shelf. I liked to put it to my ear and hear the ocean's waves. My Cha said she gave it to the pharmacist—that's Mr. Nettles."

"Would you want to see the ocean some time?"

"Oh, yes! Aunt Zarah is reading me a story about the ocean and a giant fish. Lots of things live in the water, just like on land! Someday we will all go together. But I don't want to hurt a fish, like the man in the story. Could I ride on a giant turtle?"

Rob laughed, "Sounds like a big goal, but if we find one, we have to leave it there. Cha, Zarah, Ariabella and I are blessed to have you as a part of our family. Ariabella awakes each morning looking for you."

"Mr. Rob, what about Tootsie, the doggies, my kittens, and Motoo—are they glad?"

"Very much so."

Rob pulled into the Nettles' washed-out driveway. Sheriff Curtis was there working. Sage jumped out of the truck with his toolbox and ran to the sheriff. "Mr. Sheriff Curtis, we are here to work."

Sheriff Curtis smiled and said, "Great! That's a mighty fine toolbox. Looks like you came prepared."

Rob greeted everyone and went to work rebuilding the porch. More neighbors showed up and the porch and drive were completed before dark. As Rob and Sage were set to leave, Sheriff Curtis asked Rob, "What time do you want the surprise dropped off tonight?"

"Anytime."

Sage pulled on Rob's shirt. "What surprise, my Rob? Can you tell me? Please?"

"Okay, but it's our secret," replied Rob. "You tell him, Sheriff."

"A neighbor has a male donkey he can no longer take care of. He will be a fine husband for Ariabella. What do you think? Good idea?"

Sage danced around. "Oh, yes! Ariabella told me she gets lonely by herself. She likes having the doggies around to play with, but a husband will make her very, very happy."

"Then I will bring him over tonight," said Sheriff Curtis. "Say eight o'clock?"

On the ride back, as usual, Sage was full of questions. "My Rob, what is Ariabella's new husband's name?"

"Caruso. He'll be a very good companion. I am told he loves people. Only the three of us know, so don't say anything. We will introduce him at the get together tonight in the pasture."

Night fell. The air was sultry and filled with the aroma of wet earth. Though the rains had stopped, the river had consumed possessions picked up during its rampage: lawn chairs, picnic tables, bikes, cars, homes, outbuildings, and the sadness of washed-away graves.

Rob said, "After the party, we'll get a good night's rest. We must give as much assistance as possible to our neighbors. Some folks lost everything."

"I understand, my Rob. Having nothing doesn't feel good. We have so much happiness; there is more than enough to share with our neighbors. Did I work well on the porch?"

"You sure did, and what a quick learner! Thanks, Sage." Sage glowed from hearing Rob's praise.

When they returned, Cha looked at their dirty clothes and said, "You are covered in Georgia red clay mud, but so handsome. Now get cleaned up for the party, and Sage you can tell us all about your day."

CHAPTER TWENTY-TWO

Rainbow's End

After the rains, the pasture had come alive with wildflowers. Cha picked bunches and placed them in lavender and blue jars, adorning the table under the stately tree in the pasture. Rob started a fire in the rock-lined fire ring. Lanterns hanging at different levels from the tree lit up the area. Zarah's special strawberry sweet tea and great food, including a large coconut cake, filled a long wooden table.

Tootsie's cage sat close by on a haystack. Motoo and the kittens curled up together on a soft blanket. Feed buckets were full and tied with balloons, along with a bunch of alfalfa—Ariabella's favorite food. Ruby and Lady seemed most interested in chasing fireflies with Sage. Ariabella couldn't figure out who she was. She would imitate the dogs and cats, and would even try to sit on the table, which gave everyone a great laugh.

After eating, Zarah spoke, "I would like to share my plans with all of you. The old bank building is up for sale. It's perfect for a gem and jewelry shop. It will also be an inn, my home, and workshop. With Rob's aesthetic eye, it will be so special. Rob can use the hundred acres on the river as he desires. We talked about having canoe tours and walking trails, but that will be his choice. I am looking forward to living in the village."

Cha stood and lifted her glass. "Here's to my new neighbor and friend, and 'starting overs.'"

Rob called to Sage to join everyone at the table. When Sage ran up, Rob said, "Sage, I have a big surprise, but first I have to give another confirmation to Cha." Rob continued, "I am honored to be your future husband, to share my life with you and Sage. Zarah made you a ring a few days after she met you. She had a feeling we were predestined." He reached into his pocket and handed Cha a turquoise and diamond ring inscribed, "My heart, Rob."

Zarah said, "Rob knows I would give my life for him. I am so proud of the man he's become. Now I will have my Cha as a daughter and Sage as my grandchild. Thanks, son. It is with the greatest joy I toast this incredible family you brought into my life." Zarah choked up.

Cha slipped the ring on her finger and hugged Rob. "Thank you, both. It's beautiful." Sage walked over to them and joined in the hug. Rob let go of Cha and picked up Sage.

"My Rob," Sage said, "does this mean you'll never leave us?"

"Sage, I won't promise I will never go away, but I will always come home," Rob said with emotion in his voice.

Sage wiggled from Rob's arms and said, "I have to tell all of our animal family we have a father." He told Tootsie, Calico, and Beau. Then he ran into the pasture to catch up with Ariabella.

"Hey Sage, bring Ariabella over here. Sheriff Curtis will be here soon with our surprise," Rob called.

Cha, radiant with happiness, noticed that Zarah's shoulders drooped.

"Everything okay?"

"I'm tired," Zarah said. "All this excitement. Excuse me while I go in and rest. You can tell me about the surprise later."

Headlights announced the arrival of the sheriff's truck that pulled a horse trailer. Beams of light shot across the pasture where Cha stood. Cha smiled and moved closer to Ariabella, giving her a tight squeeze around the neck.

Cha whispered in the donkey's ear, "I'm guessing this has something to do with you."

Ariabella's ears went back. She could smell the new arrival in the air and raised her head high. She trotted toward the fence where the sheriff stood holding the halter of the proud-looking Caruso. Rob opened the gate and Caruso entered the pasture. Aria took off at a gallop to the other side of the pasture, stopped, and threw up her heels. Caruso watched and waited.

Sage was delighted, but not forgetting his manners said, "Thank you very much, Mr. Sheriff. Would you like something to eat or drink?"

"Don't mind if I do," Sheriff Curtis said. "It's been a long, hard day. So many folks still need assistance. The damage from the flood was great, but we are blessed no one was hurt. Things can be replaced. Rob, you have been the driving force for getting help to our neighbors."

Cha gave Sheriff Curtis a hug and said, "We thought of setting up tents in the pasture, with food and supplies for anyone still in need. Maybe some music would lift their spirits."

"You bet!" said Sheriff Curtis. "I'll help any way I can."

"Please come join our happy celebration. Rob and I are getting married. Zarah's health is improving and she is moving into the village. And you've brought Ariabella a mate! "We will get the license as soon as possible, and one for our four-footed newlyweds. Are you a notary, Sheriff Curtis?"

"Yes!"

Sage laughed so hard, he fell on the grass.

Sheriff Curtis looked around. "Rob, where's Zarah? She all right? Does she need anything?"

"She is resting at the moment, but she will be glad you asked about her."

Sheriff Curtis could not hold back his emotion. "Do you know I was always in love with your mother? In high school, we dated a few times and were great pals. I asked her to marry me when she became pregnant. Unfortunately for me, you are not my child. I would've married her under any circumstances, but Zarah didn't want marriage. I went on to marry my lovely wife, Lanie. Our marriage is solid. Zarah knows I would be here for her if she needed me. I would have been proud to be your father, Rob."

Rob squeezed his arm around the sheriff's shoulder. "I feel the same with respect for you."

"By the way, those two troublesome brothers have been a great help cleaning up the roads. Any time you need them to work on their debt, Miss Cha, they are ready—handyman chores, whatever you need."

Cha said, "That's good news. Thanks for letting me know."

"So long! See you all at the double wedding!"

Cha placed a quilt close to the fire ring. Sage joined her. Rob poured two glasses of champagne and handed one to Cha.

Cha said, "This has been an unforgettable night. I wanted to wait for Zarah, but she will understand. No champagne for me for about nine months. I'm pregnant."

Sage picked up Calico and Beau, rose from the grass and started to dance, shouting, "I am going to be a big brother to Saffron and Cinnamon!"

Rob and Cha laughed with joy. Rob kissed her, pulled her hair back, and whispered private words.

Sage joined them, and Cha gathered him into her arms, kittens and all. Sage said, "I am so happy! I will be the best big brother and protect the twins."

A tear rolled down Cha's cheek and she asked, "Sage, are you sure we are having twins?"

"I am sure, my Cha! Saffron and Cinnamon are eager to join us! Why are you crying?"

"They are tears of happiness."

Rob was thrilled to see Sage so excited. Rob said, "Sage, no two girls will be more welcomed or blessed to have you as a brother. The names are perfect."

Full of bliss, the ecstatic family lay back onto the quilt and fell silent. Rob's two dogs, along with Motoo, the kittens, Tootsie, as well as Ariabella and Caruso joined them. A lone firefly blinked his approval.

Rob said, "I bet Ariabella and Caruso will have baby news for us, too. Maybe more twins."

Sage giggled.

Cha said, "Let's put out the fire and clean up tomorrow."

"We'll do it, Cha," Rob said. "We'll meet you inside. Sage, help me with the animals."

Cha kissed them both and walked toward the cottage. She paused for a moment to give thanks for her new life. She raised her face to heaven and said, "Father, you were right, I found my rainbow's end. My journey to Divine brought unexpected blessings. Phenomenal people and animals have entered my life. They inspire me each day, as I do them."

She looked at the stars, and then continued. "Remembering no longer causes me sorrow. I know you and Mother loved me, and I am the person I am now because of where I came from. When I plant an herb in my garden—tenderly, as you taught me, Father—I am guided by your hand. When I admire and caress an antique table I've purchased, Mother's hand guides me. I like to believe you are both in a serene place, and on occasion, that you hold hands and walk barefoot in the rich soil of the gardens above." She giggled, envisioning that scene in heaven.

When everyone was in the cottage, Cha felt engulfed in a sense of well-being. She pulled the soft, sweet kittens in close. Motoo brushed against her leg. The dogs were by her side and Tootsie quieted for the night. Sage played with the dogs and Dino on the floor while Zarah slumbered in an easy chair. Rob gave Cha a Rhett Butler kiss. All felt right.

*"There are no extra pieces in the universe.
Everyone is here because he or she has a place to fill,
and every piece must fit itself into
the big jigsaw puzzle."*

—*Deepak Chopra*

About the Author

J erry Brown Schwartz grew up on a farm in Smyrna, GA. She moved to New York as a young woman, but was always and remained a Southern Girl. She has always loved stories, and knew someday she would write books. She is now the author of two previous books, *So Inspired: Preludes and Poems* (for which she earned an honorable mention from the Self-Published Book Awards) and *Charlie Purple Turnipseed and The Dixie Brood*. She lives in Georgia and North Carolina with her husband Harry.